PUFFIN BOOKS

Castaway Kids

D0514517

Pat Hewitt

Castaway Kids

Illustrated by
Christopher Inns

PUFFIN BOOKS

PUFFIN BOOKS

Published by the Penguin Group
Penguin Books Ltd, 27 Wrights Lane, London w8 5TZ, England
Penguin Books USA Inc., 375 Hudson Street, New York, New York 10014, USA
Penguin Books Australia Ltd, Ringwood, Victoria, Australia
Penguin Books Canada Ltd, 10 Alcorn Avenue, Toronto, Ontario, Canada M4V 3B2
Penguin Books (NZ) Ltd, 182–190 Wairau Road, Auckland 10, New Zealand

Penguin Books Ltd, Registered Offices: Harmondsworth, Middlesex, England

Published in Puffin Books 1994
1 3 5 7 9 10 8 6 4 2

Text copyright © Pat Hewitt, 1994
Illustrations copyright © Christopher Inns, 1994
All rights reserved

The moral right of the author has been asserted

Thanks to Harry Page, *Daily Mirror*, for the use of his photography

Filmset by Datix International Limited, Bungay, Suffolk
Printed in England by Clays Ltd, St Ives plc
Set in 11/14 pt Monophoto Imprint

Except in the United States of America, this book is sold subject
to the condition that it shall not, by way of trade or otherwise, be lent,
re-sold, hired out, or otherwise circulated without the publisher's
prior consent in any form of binding or cover other than that in
which it is published and without a similar condition including this
condition being imposed on the subsequent purchaser

for Craig, Matthew and Stacey Williams
(who lived through this)

Contents

Is your dad Indiana Jones?

Mum and Dad had gone away. Dad had taken unpaid leave from work and they'd decided to set off round the world, looking, so the children were told, for a desert island on which to live for a while. Stacey didn't understand much about this, but you couldn't blame her. She was the baby – only a year and two months old when Mum and Dad left. It certainly made her restless for a time: at night she didn't want to go to sleep, and she fussed even more than usual about her food. But in time Stacey settled down. Their Nanna had come to live with them and they all loved their Nanna.

Matthew was four. He understood that his parents' holiday would be a long one. Dad had told him he'd always dreamt of living on an island, and now he and Mum wanted to try it for real. Matthew's imagination strained to make a picture of the island, but it wouldn't come together. He'd been told it was part of the Cook Islands, which he thought meant it must be inhabited by cooks in white aprons and tall hats such as he'd seen on television advertisements and in cartoons. But, apart from this, he had no very definite idea of a desert island. The place where his parents had gone was about as clear in his mind as some place out of last night's faded dream.

Of the three of them, Craig was the oldest. At eight, he knew that the Cook Islands were a very long way away, on the other side of the world. Craig's personal idea of a desert island was concise: a mound of sand (that was the desert part) surrounded by a wide and empty sea (the island part). Standing in the middle of the island was a solitary palm tree, under which Mum and Dad spent their days sitting in ragged trousers and bare feet, waving a flag for any passing ships to rescue them. Or maybe putting a message in a bottle and casting it adrift. The message would say *HELP*. Eventually, Craig reasoned, someone would pick up the bottle, read the message and send a rescue expedition. Not until then would his parents come home. It might take time, but it would happen sooner or later. Nanna said it would happen by Christmas.

Maybe the bottle would come bobbing all the way home to Swansea, which was where the children lived. The beach was a short walk down the hill from West Cross, the estate where their house was, and when the tide went out there was plenty of exposed sand for the bottle to land on. Craig didn't go down to the shore all that often, but, when he did, he always secretly had a look around for his dad's message bottle. He never found it though.

When Craig told the kids at school, they were pretty interested. As far as he could tell, the teachers just thought it was peculiar for Mum and Dad to go off like that. *Eccentric* was another word they used. But Craig's classmates wanted to know a lot more about the trip. Their interest was well expressed by a boy named Paul, who one day ran up to Craig in the playground during break.

'Hey, Craig,' he said. 'Is your dad Indiana Jones?'

2

The idea of adventure – Indiana Jones-type adventure – appealed to the kids at Craig's school. Real true adventure meant going away into the unknown, exploring parts of the world where there were no people, or else the people lived by strange laws and customs that would make your hair stand on end. This type of adventure also involved battling against storms and earthquakes, facing ferocious animals, suffering from insect bites and thirst, catching malaria, yellow fever and scurvy.

Some of them had read that in very cold climates, such as you find in Antarctica, your toes fall off one by one from frostbite. Intense desert heat, on the other hand, can give you sunstroke, dehydration and delirium. In the delirium you stand on top of the dunes and see distant oases overflowing with clear, cool, blue water and shaded by lush trees. Your parched throat gives out a croak of excitement and you take off down the slope of the dune, stumbling towards the beautiful sight. However, when at last you approach the place where you thought you'd seen the water, there is nothing there. These oases are only cruel mirages in the bone-dry sand.

Craig was not frightened by all this. Sometimes at night, lying in bed before he slept, he longed for his parents to return in time for morning. Most children like to have presents when their parents come back from a trip, but to Craig the presents didn't matter. It didn't matter if they failed to bring a single thing back with them, just so long as they came back themselves. But he never doubted that one day they *would* return and so, as his Nanna said, all you needed was to be patient and brave. Christmas would soon be here and by then – for sure – Mum and Dad would be here too. That's what

3

Nanna said. She also told the children that the weather on their island was sunny and hot. So they would certainly have kept all their toes.

The day Mum and Dad came back was a fantastic day. They were deeply suntanned. Dad was full of stories about coconut palms and coloured fish and never-ending sunshine, while Mum laughed and hugged the children. Craig and Matthew were overflowing with happiness. Only little Stacey was puzzled by the two strange grown-ups who had suddenly turned up in her life. Somehow the memory of her parents had become misplaced, hidden in a tuck in Stacey's mind like a toy that gets lost among the bedclothes. So Stacey hung back at first. She wouldn't sit on her mother's knee, clinging to Nanna instead. Then, just like the missing toy that's been pushed down to the foot of the bed during the night, so, after an hour or more, Stacey located the old memories and began to act like her parents' two-year-old daughter again.

That night Craig and Matthew asked Mum and Dad if they were ever going away again.

'Yes,' said Dad. 'The island was too beautiful. It was so different from everything around here. You wouldn't believe it. So we're *definitely* going back. We've got to.'

He must have read the disappointment on his sons' faces. He smiled. 'But this time, boys, we're *all* going to go. You two, Mum, even Stacey. The whole family's going to go to the desert island. What do you think of that, eh?'

Pretending to smoke

After Christmas, Dad went back to work. Since he was nineteen, he'd been a school caretaker, and before Stacey was born the family lived at the schoolhouse of Plasmarl Junior School, in another suburb of Swansea. It had been built at the same time as the school itself and stood beside the playground. There was a lady just across the road who was so old she could remember the school and schoolhouse back at the turn of the century. In her young days the local people used to beg the caretaker to give them the burning cinders from the school boiler for their fires, they were so hard up. Nowadays, it was the schoolhouse that was going through tough times. It had no proper heating of its own and was infested with mice. Mum, Dad and the two boys ended up living in just the one downstairs room until, at last, the Plasmarl school-house was condemned as unfit, and Dad moved to a new job.

After that, instead of having one school to look after, Dad had a pair of them, a quarter of a mile apart. This meant he was always buzzing like a madman between the two primary schools, on his push-bike, trying to get everything done. He did a lot of worrying. If there were not enough toilet rolls it was his fault. If the boilers stopped boiling or the Hoovers stopped hoovering, he was blamed. Dad took security very much to heart.

There was so much crime in South Wales, and with schools being so full of valuable property – computers and the like – he was hard pressed to keep the burglars out. The children thought of their dad as almost a lawman. He was in charge of a gigantic ring of keys. He had chased thieves through the corridors of the schools. He waged a constant war against paint-spray tagging and graffiti on the walls.

That, he told them, was life in modern Britain: a place which was defaced and dirty, a place where everything had to be locked up and you could hardly trust anyone; a place, basically, that wasn't nice to live or grow up in. Not like the desert island, where life couldn't help being simple, clean and honest. And, what's more, you didn't need any cash.

But you needed cash to get there, that was for sure. Thousands of pounds, it was going to cost. That was why Dad's accident was such a blow. It meant he couldn't work again.

The school had just bought a new floor-polishing machine – known as the Buffer – and it weighed heavy. One morning Dad was dragging this monster up the stairs by himself, when he suddenly felt something in his back go click. The pain was instant, like an electric shock. He let go of the Buffer and it crashed back down the steps while Dad lurched sideways and clung to the banister rail. He couldn't move at all and had to wait until somebody came.

Later they phoned to tell Mum that he'd done his back in so badly that they'd taken him to hospital. He stayed there for twenty-four hours before being transferred back home, but for weeks he could only lie on the floor, trying

6

to ease the constant pain with breathing exercises he'd learned doing Japanese aikido. Eventually the pain eased off, but Dad never went back to work. They put him on a pension, although it wasn't much money at all.

So now the family had a problem. Where were they going to get the funds they needed to return – all together, this time – to the South Seas?

Mum and Dad had never been smokers. But one night Dad surprised everyone by saying that he wished he was, because then he could pack it in and keep the money saved in a biscuit tin. So Mum said, why don't they pretend they *did* smoke, and then pretend to give up? So, overnight, they both became imaginary ex-twenty a day smokers, trudging up to the attic every night to 'pay' their fag money into an old biscuit tin. After all, they reasoned, a lot of people do smoke, and however poor they are they always somehow find the cash to do it. The Williams family would do the same. Eventually that biscuit tin was full to the brim with cash – but it was still a long way short of being enough to finance a trip for five people halfway round the world.

Mum said there was nothing for it: the whole family would have to start selling their belongings piece by piece. First the hi-fi system went and the collection of CDs. Mum started going to car-boot sales with her friend Jane, getting up at five-thirty in the morning to secure a good pitch. That was how she sold the hedge-cutter, the electric kettle, the surplus clothes, the ornaments, the books, Dad's mountain bike and her own bike. She sold most of the pictures, including the big one in the living-room with the clock-tower in it. Stacey's pushchair, too, had to go, followed by Craig's Sega games console. Matthew's red BMX and the TV in the boys' bedroom. In this way they all made difficult sacrifices. Stacey's tricycle had been given her that lovely Christmas when Mum and Dad had come home. Now she had to say goodbye to it again. She didn't want to. She shouted and screamed and wouldn't let go of the handlebars. In the end her fingers had to be prised free.

Because he wasn't working, Dad spent a lot of time looking at maps and thinking about the South Seas. To the kids the islands just looked like tiny dots, no bigger than pinpricks, in the huge expanse of the Pacific Ocean. Dad got books from the library about the Cook Islands and read passages from them out loud. He also wrote a lot of letters, because, even when they *did* get the money together for their tickets, they couldn't just set off for blue water without some forward planning. There were people he and Mum had already met out in the Cook Islands, and the children heard in particular the names of William Richards and Kuraka-Kuraka, important men whose friendship would be needed to help arrange the new trip. Fresh permissions were required from the authorities on Rarotonga, where the government and the parliament of the whole island group were established. You couldn't simply turn up and pitch your tent.

Dad also had the idea that the media might help them. The family had made contact with a local radio reporter, Caroline Sarll, and the story of Mum and Dad's first journey had been broadcast and written about locally, including in the pages of the *Swansea Evening Post*. One day there was great excitement. The telephone rang and a voice spoke with a lazy, London accent.

'Hello, Mr Williams? I'm ringing you from the *Daily*

Mirror in London. We were wondering if we could do a story about your trip to the Pacific Ocean.'

The *Daily Mirror*! London! The national daily papers, they knew, had a lot more money than the local press. Maybe they could do a deal. Mum and Dad would receive a bit of help in getting money for the fares in return for the family giving their story.

In the end there was some sort of deal with the *Mirror*. It wasn't a huge sum, but when added to what they'd already scraped together Dad knew he had enough to buy the tickets. He was very cheerful. It looked as if, after two years of struggle, his plans were about to bear fruit.

He immediately sat down to work out when they should leave. Once they'd got Christmas out of the way – that would be a good time to kick the dust of Swansea off their shoes, they all thought. Right, January was the month, or February at the latest. Dad telephoned the travel agent to inquire about air tickets. At last, they were on their way.

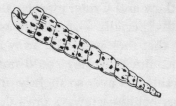

3

Good night, Charlie

So Christmas came round, the fourth since Mum and Dad had returned from the South Seas. The weather in Wales was cold and frosty. They had little money to spare for presents and feasting, but the family was cheered by the thought of the hot, high summer waiting for them on the other side of the world. In only four weeks, Mum told the children, they'd have burning white sand between their toes, a sweltering sun on their heads and a deep blue horizon, straight and flat, surrounding them. The departure date on the airline tickets was 6 February.

The children's excitement was growing, but it was a muted excitement. All through January they attended school as usual, knowing they would not see the end of term. To Matthew and Craig, moments spent with their friends seemed especially significant, as the realization began to dawn that they would be away from home for a long, long time. But still they could not get rid of that feeling that all this was ever so slightly unreal. Moving to the South Seas, being castaways on a desert island, was what happened only in books, or on *Blue Peter*, or to the families of explorers and adventurers. They still had a little trouble seeing Dad as Indiana Jones, even though they both had Welsh names.

For instance, what did Indiana Jones do with the

family pets when he went on expeditions? Maybe he didn't have any pets, but Craig, Matthew and Stacey did. First there was the dog, Webster, a Yorkshire terrier with short legs and a coat of long, shiny, straight hair which brushed the ground as he walked. Webster had become rather a handful, growling and then snapping at fingers and ankles without warning. Mum was concerned he might end up biting Stacey, so Webster was found another home.

The next problem was Roger, who, being a rabbit, lived in a hutch just inside the back door. He had a fluffy, pure white coat, watery pink eyes and a most placid disposition. Everybody in the family rather loved Roger and only reluctantly did they accept that he would have to be given away. When Mum suggested Casey, the seven-year-old granddaughter of their next-door neighbour, that seemed a good way of keeping in touch with their pet, at least a little bit. Craig was particularly cut up about giving up the rabbit. When Casey's dad came round to pick up Roger, he gave a last, loving stroke to his flattened-down velvet ears and lowered him carefully into the cardboard carrying-box. He had punched holes in the sides of the box so that Roger wouldn't suffocate. He would miss Roger.

Finally there was the problem of what to do with Charlie. He was a goldfish, won by Craig and Dad throwing darts at a fair in Mumbles. Originally there had been two fish, but Charlie's bowl-mate, Jaws, had recently died, leaving poor Charlie to circulate his bowl alone. Craig approached his friend David, who agreed to take Charlie to lodge with him. Craig said he would take the fish round on the day before they left.

A sharpish reminder of what lay ahead came when they went down to the doctor's for their immunization jabs. These were against evil-sounding diseases like typhoid, tetanus and hepatitis, and the process required two injections in the arm and one in the rump. Mum held Stacey as her skin was being swabbed down with surgical spirit, and everything was fine until Stacey saw the needle glinting between the fingers of the practice nurse. Then she started to twist and pull away from Mum, the tears bursting from her eyes.

'No! No!' she screamed.

'You won't be able to go to the island, Stacey, if you don't have the injection,' Mum told her.

'Well, I don't *want* to go to the island. I don't want to GO! I don't want to GO!'

The nurse gave Mum a funny look. The whole waiting-room must have heard Stacey's screams about this island to which she did not want, at *any* price, to go.

After the ordeal was over, Mum took them to Argos, where the children were told they could choose a special toy. Matthew picked two Terminators, those 'fully posable' figures based on the time-travelling robot played by Arnold Schwarzenegger. Stacey came away with a blonde-haired doll, which she promptly christened Sarah. But Craig said he would like five pounds to spend somewhere else.

There was plenty to distract Craig in those last days. He was a member of the Swansea Youth Theatre, and they were rehearsing a big production of *Bugsy Malone*, the play about gangsters and their molls fighting over a consignment of deadly splatterguns. Craig had been given the part of one of Bugsy's henchmen, Babyface. The show's last performance was due to take place in front of a sell-out audience at the Grand Theatre, Swansea, on the night before their departure. They would all be there – his parents, Nanna and Bampa, his uncle Alun, and loads of their friends.

Meanwhile Dad took them to Millets in town, where they bought a tent, cooking pots and sleeping-bags. At the last moment Dad picked out a big electric torch encased in rubber.

'We'll be needing this,' said Dad. 'It'll be dark on the island at night. There's only the moon.' He spoke almost reluctantly. He didn't want to take any more reminders of modern city life than they had to.

'The point is to be self-contained and live off the island,' he'd already told them. 'We don't want a radio or medicines and we're not taking any food with us. We're going to eat what we find out there and have as few reminders of the twentieth century as we can.'

He told the children to choose a rucksack each, in which they would carry their personal things. For days after that Craig, Matthew and Stacey agonized over what to take with them. Craig, who'd recently started at the comprehensive school, had been given a mountain of schoolwork to keep him up to the mark while he was away. Alongside this he packed Bank Raid, the hand-held computerized game he'd bought with his five pounds, and Perfection, a battery-operated game which tests the speed of your brain and your hand. Finally he included his copy of *Charlie and the Chocolate Factory*. There would be no chocolate on the island, his father told him. Well, at least he could read about it.

In his packing, Matthew remained faithful to the

collection of men, the main elements of most of his games. As well as the new Terminator, he packed three Action Force characters, code-named Snake-eyes, Fireball and Jerrycan. He also included the figure of Luke Skywalker from *Star Wars*, a couple of Ewoks from the same film and a Monster-in-my-Pocket.

Stacey packed and unpacked her rucksack several times a day, trying to decide what was essential. Sarah the new doll could not be left out, of course. Finally she settled on a jigsaw, a couple of games in boxes, a picture book or two and some paper and crayons for drawing. The toys that were left behind were boxed up and put away in the attic.

It turned out that they needed the rubber torch sooner than expected – even before they left home. With just two days to go, the men from the gas and electricity came to switch off their supplies. Then the whole family began to understand how harsh the British winter can be. Night came by four o'clock and all they had were the torches and candles to give light. There was no heat and they ate only cold pies and sandwiches and – for a treat – fish and chips from Dick Barton's fish shop down the road. The weather was icy. So was the washing-up water.

It all became too much for Charlie the goldfish. Perhaps it was the sudden drop in temperature, perhaps it was the sight of humans preparing for departure outside his bowl. Whatever it was, Charlie did not see it through. When Matthew went to feed him on the last day, he found him floating lifeless on his side on the surface of his water. There was nothing much you could say, except good night, Charlie, and nothing much to do except give him a decent burial in the rose-bed. And this they did.

4

Get Babyface!

So the last day dawned, dusked and became dark. Two suitcases stood at the bottom of the stairs with three plump rucksacks beside them. Dad was going round locking the windows.

The plan was to secure the house, go down to the Grand Theatre with Dad's brother Alun to see Craig perform, and then spend the night at the house of Mum and Dad's friends Gareth and Jane. Gareth had offered to drive them to Cardiff the next morning, from where they would catch the five past seven train to London. Once in London they'd take another train to Gatwick Airport.

Craig, preparing for his part in the play, had little time to think about the long train and plane journey ahead, even though it would be the first time he had ever flown. For months now Craig had been living half inside the world of hoodlums from Chicago, and their speakeasies and gang rivalry. As Babyface in *Bugsy Malone* he would be wearing a flat tweed cap and baggy white shirt, which they'd borrowed from Gareth. His face was smeared with mud to make it grubby and unrespectable. As Joe the Barman, his other part, Craig had a black waistcoat and a spotted bow-tie, which belonged to Bampa.

Rehearsals had gone well, and they had already done two performances which the director had also praised.

'But you can all do even better. Tonight's the last performance. Give it all you've got, OK?'

Craig gave it all he'd got. Babyface was not one of the star characters, but he was fun to play. When he wasn't on stage, Joe usually was, working the bar at the speakeasy, where much of the action happens. On balance, Craig preferred Babyface. He was one of Bugsy's trusted men, though none too clever as it happened. Craig's favourite bit was naturally where he got his best laugh.

'Right!' Bugsy had to say at one point. 'There they are, all ready for the taking. Get Babyface.'

Leroy, standing next to his boss, jumped and barked into the ear of the next gangster, 'Get Babyface!'

There was a line of gangsters, and the instruction went along the line.

'Get Babyface . . . Get Babyface . . . Get Babyface . . .'

Finally the instruction reached Craig.

'Get Babyface!' he yelled, before realizing he was on the end of the line and had no one to pass the order to. He looked at the audience. 'Er, is there anyone called Babyface out there?'

Then he did a double take.

'What am I talking about? I *am* Babyface!'

In what seemed like no time at all, the performance was over. The lights dazzled their eyes from above and below as the actors took their bows at the front of the stage. The clapping and roaring from the happy, satisfied audience washed over them in waves. The applause was like a drug. It made Craig forget what set him apart from the rest of the cast, that he was about to exchange Wales for a lonely island halfway around the world.

At Gareth and Jane's house they didn't go to bed until midnight. In less than five hours they would be awoken, ready to start their island adventure.

Dad came in and shook Craig and Matthew awake.

'Come on, boys! Nearly five o'clock.'

Matthew crawled from his sleeping-bag and went to the window, rubbing his eyes. There was nothing to see. It was so early in the morning that it was actually still nighttime. The air was stiff with cold.

Stacey was so fast asleep that she didn't wake up until after Mum had got her dressed. They had a scratch breakfast, counted and recounted the bags, then loaded the car. Gareth scraped the ice from the windscreen.

'You'll not be seeing much of this stuff where you're going,' he commented enviously.

Dad laughed. 'There won't even be any windscreens, Gareth. There won't be any cars, or any houses, or any of this.'

He indicated the whole town with a sweep of his arm. But it was also like a wave of farewell.

And then they were gone. The car swept along the motorway as it hugged the curve of Swansea Bay, past the massive smoking steelworks of Port Talbot, the little seaside town of Porthcawl and finally Bridgend, before Gareth's car made the last twelve miles into Wales's capital city. Thinking of his triumphs the previous night, Craig still felt a little like a gangster, although he was now on the run – rising early, slipping away under cover of darkness while the law slept. 'Get Babyface!' Not if he could help it. He'd be sunning himself in Paradise before even the FBI knew he was gone.

It wasn't until they got to Cardiff railway station that things began to go wrong. The train was late departing, and they stood on the platform awkwardly, the goodbyes difficult to say. The local radio reporter, Caroline Sarll, was buzzing around with her microphone. She was asking everyone questions and they all seemed to begin *How does it feel . . .?* That was an impossible type of question to answer, really. *How* does it feel? It feels . . . just the way it feels.

Anyway, it was still too early to feel like anything in particular. The station was dull and freezing, the children, especially Stacey, were bemused by tiredness, and Mum and Dad's excitement was partly spoiled because they were getting increasingly anxious. Travel does that to you. You are faced with a string of deadlines – train departures, check-in times – and yet you depend entirely on everything going smoothly, on other people doing their jobs which you know almost nothing about. Not that you could make any difference if you did.

'MUH HUHN PHZZZ PHISSST LONDON GLOBB ZZZZTHNISSS THNUHZZZ,' said the public announcement. 'PASSENDGZZZZ DVZZZD ZZZVAYN VRUHSTUHL.'

'What was that?' Mum said. 'Something about London. What did they say?'

'THISSAULT MMN-MMN SQUEEKOMSTAN-SES ONDARKUMTROLE. BLOOTUSHRAY WAH-WAHGRETZ.'

Dad went to find out. He asked a railwayman. The children could see the man shaking his head, eyes wide open. Dad lifted his arms, his hands stretched, then dropped them back to his sides – a gesture of disbelief. He returned.

'Train's been cancelled. There's flood on the line, or something. We're supposed to take the Bristol train in an hour and change. We can't get to London until about midday or something.'

'But that'll be too late,' said Mum. 'We'll miss the flight. Come on. Let's ask again.'

They picked up their suitcases and hurried to the information counter, near the station entrance.

'We've got tickets for Gatwick, we've got a flight to catch.'

The information clerk was sympathetic.

'For passengers with urgent connections to make, British Rail will be happy to lay on a taxi service as far as Bristol. You've got an hour, so you should be able to catch the eight-fifteen InterCity to Paddington.'

It would have been ample time if they had been blessed with a taxi having a sense of urgency. As it happened, they were not so lucky, for their driver operated a personal speed-limit of forty-five miles per hour. As the distance between Cardiff and Bristol is exactly forty-five miles, and they had a mere fifty-five minutes to get there, they neatly missed the eight-fifteen by a little matter of five minutes. There was another train in an hour.

'We'll have to get a taxi across London,' Dad said, and Craig knew he was thinking about the money.

The whole expedition was being mounted on very little because, as Dad said to them, 'For six months we won't spend any money. There's no money on the island, no shops or anything. It's a totally cash-free environment, see.'

A couple of miles outside Paddington, where they were due just after eleven, the InterCity train stopped. For a long time it did nothing, neither moving forwards nor back. Dad went around some of the other passengers in the carriage, asking if they knew what the problem was. None of them did. Then came the announcement.

'British Rail regrets that, due to a security alert, Paddington station is currently closed . . .'

'What are they *talking* about?'

Dad shot a wild glance at Mum. He knew, really. A security alert meant bombs or bomb-scares and it could go on for hours. Dad tried to calm himself down by doing his yoga breathing exercises. Mum, who was naturally calm, at least on the outside, went on reading quietly to Stacey. Half an hour later the train creaked and squeaked into Paddington station.

Helter-skelter they pelted for the taxi rank. Stacey enjoyed the black London taxi in which they shuttled to Victoria, sitting on the tip-up seats with her back to the driver. At Victoria, they caught one of the mercifully frequent trains to the airport. At last, eight hours after they'd left Gareth and Jane's house and an hour before take-off, they were ready to check in.

Standing beside the Air New Zealand desk was a man in a suit, with a camera in his hand. He was almost lurking, looking around him like a sentry assessing the likely threat of an attack. As they approached the desk, the man came forward to intercept them. They knew him, of course. He'd been down in Swansea and had taken a load of pictures. The family had posed outside their school, outside their house, beside the car, beside their (still empty) suitcases, on the dirty sand of Swansea

Bay. The cameraman's name was Harry Page and he worked for the *Daily Mirror*. Harry Arnold, one of the paper's crack reporters, had also visited them at home. But Harry Arnold was not on assignment this afternoon.

'Hi, Tony,' he said to Dad. 'You're a bit late. Good journey?'

'Don't ask,' said Dad. 'Delays all the way.'

'Well, it's not too serious, there's plenty of time. Here, just line up for your check-in and I'll shoot a bit more film.'

Harry Page looked around warily before using the camera. Then, working at speed, he began to take photographs, his flashgun firing with each shot.

'I want this over quickly. Get you safely into the Departure Lounge.'

'What's the hurry?' Mum wanted to know. 'Like you said, we've got enough time.'

'Well, we've got to be careful, because I reckon there's a *Sun* photographer sniffing around looking for you.' Harry's voice was low, conspiratorial. The *Mirror* had helped Mum and Dad pay for the air tickets in return for sole rights to the family's story. The last thing they wanted now was a rival tabloid newspaper muscling in on their exclusive report.

Harry finished his photography as Dad was presenting their five air tickets and the luggage at the check-in desk. As soon as the formalities were over and boarding passes had been handed out, they said goodbye to Harry. Dad shook hands very formally and smiled his easy smile.

'We'll be seeing you in a couple of weeks or three,' said the *Mirror* man. 'Harry Arnold and I will be out to check up on how things are going, take a few pictures, et cetera.'

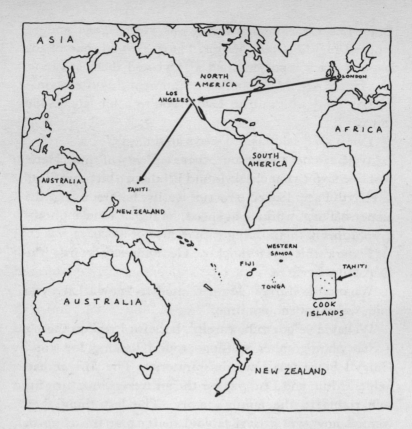

'Right,' said Dad, with his usual merry smile. 'See you then.'

He led Mum and the children between the ropes which led into Departures. Just before plunging through to the place where they X-ray the travellers and their hand-luggage, Dad turned to wave one more time. Craig, Matthew and Stacey waved too. Harry called out.

'I can't wait. Sun, sand and . . . whatever!'

Harry Page was the only one at the airport to see them off on their great adventure.

5

Raro

In their first twenty-four hours on Rarotonga, the capital of the Cook Islands, the children discovered that almost everything in the South Pacific was the opposite of what they had left behind. Looked at from this distance, Britain appeared a terribly used-up sort of place. It was cold and dark, old and scruffy, polluted; a country crowded with people who lived their lives indoors and always seemed to be crouched round the telly or arguing about money.

Rarotonga is a very small world, only twenty miles all the way around. But it seemed to Craig, Matthew and Stacey to be shiny, new and exciting. The morning air fizzed like lemonade or sherbet poppers. The children could hear wild mina birds whistling at them from the trees and, never far away, the waves breaking on the blindingly white sand. It was a sifting, bristling sound, quite different from the accompanying hollow boom of the surf as it struck against the coral reef, a few hundred metres out to sea.

The colours they saw here were as different as possible from the dull brown, mouldy grey and monochrome grass-green of wintry Swansea Bay. Here nature was coloured in with crazy scribbles, as if coming from every pen in Stacey's box of crayons – except that there were more tints of green than even the biggest colouring-box can boast. They had never imagined a bird such as the kukupa, the Cook Islands fruit dove. Its wings were of apple-green, its breast of yellow and white and it carried a flash of bright pink on the top of its head.

The way of life of the Cook Islanders was as different as possible from that of the inhabitants of the British Isles. Raro people live mostly outdoors, cooking and eating and socializing in the open air. They never wear uncomfortable clothes, always laugh a lot, and seem to enjoy the company of strangers just as much as that of old friends.

The people's lively hospitality had been obvious even at the airport. Representatives from the hotel greeted each of the arrivals with individual *ei kaki* – garlands of flowers to wear round their necks. Craig, Matthew and Stacey were enchanted by this reception. Still proudly wearing their *ei kaki*, they rode to their hotel feeling like film stars.

It was nine-thirty in the morning. The car had taken them straight to the Edgewater Resort, the modern but simple hotel whose guests slept in chalets next to the beach. First thing, after dumping their luggage, the children ran out across the sand and threw themselves into the sea. They would never have dreamt of bathing in Swansea Bay, even in summer, but this water was as pure and translucent as turquoise-stained glass turned liquid. Brilliantly coloured fish flickered and tickled around their ankles. After half an hour of tumbling and splashing in the waves, Mum and Dad came to call them back.

'We're going round to William Richards's house. Come on.'

William was a retired school inspector with whom Mum and Dad had become friends during their first journey to the Cook Islands.

'He's descended from William Marsters, an English-man from Gloucestershire,' Dad told them as they walked along the winding coastal road on the way to William's house. 'Mind you, that's nothing special. On the island where he comes from, which is called Palmerston, *everybody* is descended from William Marsters.'

'How's that, Dad?' Craig wanted to know.

'Well, Marsters was part of the crew of a whaling vessel in the middle of the last century, but he didn't like the life very much. So, when he spotted that the ship was passing close to a coral island, he jumped overboard and swam ashore. He didn't know it at the time, but he'd landed on an island with a Welsh name: Penrhyn. It was seven hundred and thirty miles north-west of here.'

'What happened when he landed? What did the people do?'

'They were savages – at least, that's what *he* would have called them. We wouldn't use that word today. But they lived in a completely different way from people in Europe.'

'Were they cannibals?'

'Maybe. There *was* cannibalism in these islands, once upon a time, I do know that.'

'What's cannibalism?' asked Stacey.

'Eating people, stupid,' said Matthew.

'Yuk,' said Stacey.

'Well, anyhow, they didn't eat William Marsters,' said Dad. 'And later he teamed up with a local man and they made a boat together. After that, Marsters was able to sail around the Cook Islands, doing a bit of trading and picking up a collection of wives. He ended up with three of them, and he took them to live with him as squatters on an uninhabited island called Palmerston, which is about two hundred and fifty miles across the ocean from here. And, in the end, Marsters was accepted as the owner and ruler of the island.'

'Wow,' said Craig. 'He must have felt like a king.'

'He had an awful lot of children and hundreds of grandchildren. His descendants are all over these islands, but on Palmerston everyone is his descendant. And the man we're going to see is one of them. When he was born he was called William Marsters, but there're so many with that name that he uses his middle name as a surname: Richards.'

William Richards's house was unlike any they had seen back home. It stood in an enormous garden, bursting with vegetation: scarlet flame trees, purple bougainvillaea, Christmas lilies, hibiscus and orchids, banana and papaw, vines, mango and breadfruit. And, of course, the coconut palm. Everywhere you looked on Rarotonga you saw coconut palms.

The house itself was a solid bungalow, self-built by William and his family. The roof was of corrugated iron, the floors rough concrete, and the whole building surrounded by a well-furnished veranda. Obviously, in this fierce, tropical, summer heat, William Richards's family did most of their living out on the veranda, where they could breathe the pure air of the South Seas and the luscious scents of the garden.

'Most of the houses are built by the people who live in them,' said Dad as they approached. 'It's a continuation of the tradition. The old-fashioned houses were made of four poles standing upright, with the walls and roof made of woven palm leaves and coconut fibre. But they didn't stand up to the hurricanes. They were just blown away.'

'Will we have hurricanes on the island, Dad?' asked Craig.

'We might, but I hope not. That's a very destructive thing, a hurricane.'

A young woman in her twenties came running out to greet them. She was smiling broadly.

'Tony! Cath! *Kia orana*. Good to see you again.'

This was Mary, William Richards's daughter. She hugged and kissed them warmly.

'Come over and say hello to my mother. Say *kia orana*.'

She laughed at Stacey's efforts to say the Maori words of greeting to Tapu Richards, who was sitting quietly in the shade of the veranda, a small woman with sparkling, humorous eyes.

After some polite inquiries about their journey, Mary went off to fetch her father, who was working in a distant part of the garden. When William appeared, a large, grey-haired man, he was carrying a fearsome instrument which looked like a cross between a butcher's chopping knife and a battle scimitar.

'What's that?' asked Stacey, after William had enthusiastically greeted them. She was pointing at the wide, curved blade.

William raised the weapon as a mock threat. Stacey flinched and William laughed. He had a husky, throaty laugh.

'Don't worry. I'm not going to eat you. This is my machete. It's for gardening and cutting down coconuts. Later I'll show you how to use it.'

Two younger members of William's family came running out of the undergrowth to inspect the blond-haired arrivals. The older, Pepe (his adopted daughter), was fourteen; his granddaughter, Marianne, was a few years younger. They both remembered Mum and Dad's visit four years ago.

Dad asked William, 'Would the children mind showing Craig, Matthew and Stacey how to collect coconuts? We'll be needing them to know.'

William spoke to Pepe and she nodded. She picked up an iron bar, sharp at each end, and the children trouped off through the garden, leaving the adults to continue their discussion of the pros and cons of various desert islands.

After a few minutes the children came to a fine, seven-metre-high palm tree, which Pepe patted as you would a favourite cow. The tree's ribbed trunk, rough as elephant's skin, rose elegantly up to the immense, quill-shaped fronds which fanned out to form a rustling green parasol high above their heads. Bunched at the top of the trunk, near the place where the stems met, were several clusters of ten or a dozen green spheres.

Pepe produced a circle of rope, which she twisted into a figure eight. Placing her feet on either side of the tree trunk, she slipped a foot into each loop of the rope and pulled it tight. Then, gripping a solid-looking stick between her teeth, she began to swarm easily upwards, using the rope to gain purchase on the ribs of the tree and so push herself higher. When she reached the top, the tautness of the rope enabled her to stand upright, with one hand free. Using the stick she had carried up with her, she poked two or three coconuts loose until they rolled free and dropped with a series of dull thuds at the feet of the watching Europeans.

Descending as smoothly as she would by lift, Pepe showed them how to husk the nut. Close to, the Williams children had only seen the nut as it appears at fairgrounds, on the coconut shy. But this looked so different – smooth and green, shaped like an oversized grape but with skin – or husk as it was called – that was thick and fibrous like banana-skin.

Pepe drove the metal bar into the ground so that it stood firm under her hands. Then, slamming the coconut down, she impaled it on the point, repeating the process until she had breached the husk in several places. Now she could begin to pull it apart with her fingers and, as she did so, the others saw that inside the skin was a

COCONUT PALMS

THE LEAVES OR FRONDS CAN BE USED FOR BASKETS, BED MATTING AND ROOF THATCHING.

THE NUT OF THE COCONUT PALM FLOATS WELL. THIS HELPS THEM SPREAD FROM ISLAND TO ISLAND.

THE TRUNK IS USED FOR BUILDING BOATS AND HOUSES AS WELL AS FOR MAKING TOOLS.

THE FRUIT OF THE COCONUT IS A READY-MADE CONTAINER AND A VALUABLE SUPPLY OF FOOD AND DRINK.

THE WHITE EDIBLE PART OF THE COCONUT. INSIDE HERE IS ALSO FOUND THE MILK

THE HARD, BROWN, HAIRY CASE OF THE COCONUT

THE FIBROUS OUTER HUSK OF THE NUT

dense layer of fibre encasing the hard shell of the nut. Finally she showed them the nut itself, stripped clean of its husk. It looked at last like the 'real' thing – the hairy brown ostrich egg, familiar to all British fairgrounds.

When they rejoined the adults, parading the nut like a prize, Dad and William Richards were deep in conversation. Dad took the coconut and turned it over in his hands.

'Back in Britain,' he said, 'I was speaking to someone about how I wanted to live on a desert island, and all he said was, "What'll you eat?" So I said, "Coconuts and fish, there's plenty of those." "You can't *just* live on coconuts and fish," he said. "You'll get malnutrition."'

William Richards shook his head.

'That is very wrong. When William Marsters first went to Palmerston Island there wasn't any other food. There was no flour or rice or sugar. William Marsters and his three wives lived on coconuts alone, and fish – and between them they raised more than thirty healthy children! Later, when traders came to sell them European stuff, they would eat that, of course. But you *can* live on coconuts. The water inside is your water. The meat is your food, as well as the pods, or sprouts, which we call *etu*. *Etu* is most delicious.'

Around the lagoon of Palmerston, two hundred and fifty miles north-west of Rarotonga, were several uninhabited *motus* or desert islands. It was on one of these that Dad was meaning to live, so the connection with William Richards was an important one. The next day, William was going to take them to meet one of the chiefs of Palmerston Island, when, after a discussion, Dad and

Mum hoped they would receive permission to go and live on one of the *motus*, known as Primrose Island.

As they were leaving to go back to the hotel, William went into his house and returned with a handbell. He rang it loudly, like a school teacher back home signalling lunchtime, and the children were delighted to see chickens come running from the undergrowth in every direction, giving loud clucks of anticipation.

William chuckled. 'These hens are mostly wild, you know. I feed them, and then later they feed me. They're much more sweet to eat than the imported chickens which most people have. Much nicer.'

Then they shook hands and said *aere ra* to William and Tapu.

'We shall meet again tomorrow,' said William. 'I shall take you to the Parliament House, where you shall meet John James Marsters, the Headman of Palmerston Island and its lagoon. You must discuss your request to go there. He must agree.'

6

Seeing the Headman

'O Lord, in thy mercy, grant wisdom to these deliberations and lead us along the path of righteousness and truth.'

The scene was a meeting room at the Rarotonga Parliament House, where two Cook Islanders were sitting with inclined heads, their eyes closed. The one who led the prayer was John James Marsters, one of the Headmen of the island and lagoon of Palmerston. He was a white-haired man in his sixties. The other was a member of the Cook Islands central government. Mum, Dad and William Richards sat opposite, heads likewise bowed.

Then John James straightened up and looked sternly across the table at the visitors from Wales. His voice was firm.

'So, to our business. Would you please explain to us, Mr Williams, exactly *why* you wish to take your children to live on Primrose Island in the Palmerston lagoon?'

Dad glanced at William, who made a minute nod of the head. Dad cleared his throat to reply.

'Well, it's like this, you see . . .'

When they'd all arrived in Rarotonga, Mum and Dad still hadn't decided exactly which desert island they wanted to settle on. Their first trip, four years ago, had been to Takutea, a low and tiny sandbank ten miles across the shark-infested ocean from the nearest settlement and more than a hundred from Rarotonga. But they knew that Takutea was too isolated and, in a hurricane, too dangerous a place to take children, for at its highest point it was only two metres above sea level. On this trip, they would have to make another choice.

The fifteen Cook Islands are scattered over one and a quarter million square miles of ocean, but they include only twelve inhabited settlements. Almost all of them are atolls – that is, patches of shallow ocean ringed by coral reefs which originally formed millions of years ago out of massive volcanic eruptions. Having erupted, the volcanoes sank back below the surface of the sea but left behind lagoons in the same shape as the original volcanic craters. Outside the barrier of coral reef lies the untamed Pacific Ocean, more than six miles down at its deepest. But

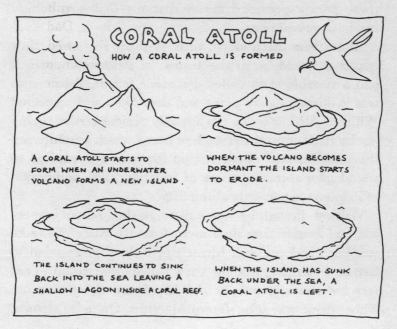

CORAL ATOLL
HOW A CORAL ATOLL IS FORMED

A CORAL ATOLL STARTS TO FORM WHEN AN UNDERWATER VOLCANO FORMS A NEW ISLAND.

WHEN THE VOLCANO BECOMES DORMANT THE ISLAND STARTS TO ERODE.

THE ISLAND CONTINUES TO SINK BACK INTO THE SEA LEAVING A SHALLOW LAGOON INSIDE A CORAL REEF.

WHEN THE ISLAND HAS SUNK BACK UNDER THE SEA, A CORAL ATOLL IS LEFT.

within the lagoons the water is calm and generally no more than a dozen metres deep. Thanks to the barrier reef and the shallow water, sharks don't venture inside the lagoon. The water is generally clear and well-behaved.

Most lagoons have one main island, where the people live. Sometimes it's a rocky mountain which occupies the centre of the lagoon, like Rarotonga. Sometimes, though, it is not much more than a big mound of sand and volcanic earth, Palmerston being an example of this type. In most cases there are also a number of small, deserted islets – *motus* – scattered around the edge of the reef circle. They are scarcely more than sandbanks, planted only with palm trees and scrub and home to nothing except sea-birds, lizards and crabs. But it was on one of these poorly provided *motus* that the Williams family meant to go and live.

After their discussions with William Richards, they hoped it would be in the lagoon of Palmerston, which had a suitable *motu* called Primrose Island. Palmerston was William's native place and they liked and respected William. Also, it was a particularly remote lagoon, being out by itself amid the stretch of ocean which lies between the Cook Islands' northern and southern groups, and so would give a greater sense of isolation. The population of Palmerston was only about fifty.

William, though he was a distinguished school inspector, had lived a long time away from the place where he was born and couldn't himself give them permission to live on Primrose. But he knew a man who could. That was his relation, one of the Headmen of Palmerston, whose name was John James Marsters. Quite by chance,

John James happened to be in Rarotonga right now for a course of medical treatment. So William Richards took Mum, Dad and the children down to a prearranged meeting with his distinguished relative and the government man, who had asked to be there also. William sat in on their discussions.

In trying to explain himself, Dad told John James about pollution in South Wales. He told him about the pace of life, the desperate unemployment, the crime and unhappiness, the suicide statistics. Above all, he mentioned the materialism of life.

'Everybody's struggling with everybody else, see. There's an expression: dog-eat-dog. That describes our culture in Britain. It's very stressful, very unnatural and restless. The whole society concentrates on money and power. I think that's corrupting. I mean, I want my children to experience nature, a life of nature, for themselves. Something pure and not corrupt, because that's not a suitable type of atmosphere to be growing up in. Anyway, that's what we think.'

At that point Mum broke in. She felt the argument needed something practical to back it up.

'The two of us, Tony and me, were out here four years ago, on Takutea. So we know what it's like. And we've brought schoolwork with us for the children: books, writing materials. We'll be teaching them ourselves, so they won't miss out on their education.'

This was a long speech, coming from Mum. John James nodded, appreciative of her obvious sincerity. Then the minister had a question.

'You mean to stay permanently on the *motu*?'

'No, sir, not permanently,' said Dad.

He looked at Mum; she smiled. Then he faced the minister again.

'We'll stay as long as possible, though. I mean, as long as we can.'

There was a pause. John James turned to William and they began a murmured conversation in Maori, while Mum and Dad waited tensely. This was it. Mum and Dad had made their pitch, stated their case, and there was nothing more they could do. In the next few minutes it would be decided whether this journey, halfway round the world, had been an utter waste of time and money. If they were forced to return to Swansea now, it would be in failure, their tails between their legs. There was no possibility of staying without the desert island, because they had no money. Dad had explained it to the children back home, before they started. On Primrose they would live off the land and the sea. There'd be no need for cash, because there was nothing to buy. But the little money they had would quickly run out if they had to stay on in Rarotonga as tourists.

And suppose they had to go back now? Dad could just hear the carping comments from all those who had doubted them: *What did we tell them? Never get away with it, that's what. Can't just go off into the blue-yonder* ... He didn't look forward to the humiliation.

At the beginning, after they'd been introduced and said *kia orana*, the children had been told to go outside and explore the Parliament gardens. After that, the adults' deliberations had been punctuated by the sound of Craig, Matthew and Stacey playing chase, their screams of laughter ringing out from between the trees and across the grass. They sounded happy, at ease, full of life.

Dad looked at the two men, deep in consultation, nodding their heads in unison. They seemed to have reached a conclusion at last. Mum and Dad held their breath as John James turned back to them.

'OK, Mr and Mrs Williams. Your reasons for going to the island are good. I will give you the permission you need. You *may* go and live on Primrose Island. There will be no charge.'

Dad's face lit up. His eyes sparkled. He was about to jump to his feet and start thanking John James profusely. But the Headman stopped him, holding his hand up like a traffic cop.

'There are two conditions. First, if you write about the island and the islanders after this period on Primrose *motu*, you must tell the truth. There have been too many people spreading bad stories about us. You must only write the truth.'

Mum and Dad nodded their heads. They had read some of these lies themselves. People had even said, libellously, that dogs were eaten in the Cook Islands.

'Yes, I agree,' said Dad. 'What is the other condition?'

'We are a very Christian people, Mr Williams. Our founder, William Marsters, was a God-fearing man. Therefore we do not allow any bathing whatsoever on a Sunday.'

7

Cannibals and missionaries

When they saw Mum and Dad emerging from the meeting, the children ran towards them across the grass. Before he had covered half the distance, Matthew had seen the look in Dad's eyes. He knew that they were going to the island.

'Yes,' said Dad. 'Permission is granted. We can go to Primrose.'

So they would not, after all, be forced back to Swansea with only a few days of tourism on Rarotonga to their credit. They had their desert island. The dream was coming true, and surely nothing could stop them now.

Or could it?

As they were about to learn, arrangements in the South Pacific rarely go smoothly or according to plan, especially when you want to travel to the less populated islands. Even today, few of the atolls have airstrips and movement between them by sea is haphazard. Several freighters carry goods and passengers around the islands, but their sailings are always being disrupted or cancelled. The ships are old. They frequently break down and most of them, sooner or later, get wrecked on one of the reefs.

So when it turned out that there was no boat leaving for Palmerston for at least five weeks, Mum and Dad were nearly in despair. How could they stay in Rarotonga for *five weeks*? For one thing, their money would run out.

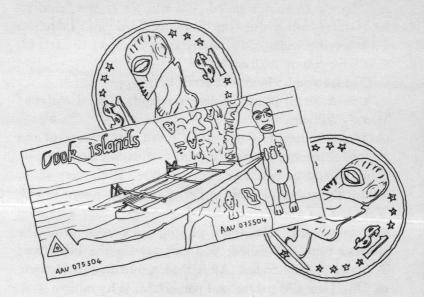

And, what was worse, the two men from the *Daily Mirror* were due to come in only a fortnight, eagerly expecting to find the Williams family camping out in a solitary demi-paradise all of their own. They could hardly print an article about Mum, Dad and the kids making sandcastles on the beach outside the Edgewater Resort Hotel.

Islanders, being well used to travel setbacks, have a relaxed knack of switching off their impatience. Dad, however, had not yet acquired it. Actually, he reckoned he couldn't afford to.

'What am I going to do?' he groaned to William Richards, later that day. 'I've got to get on a desert island soon. I've *got* to.'

William, though, was nothing if not a practical man

39

and he had an immediate solution.

'There's an island called Aitutaki. It is one hundred and thirty miles due north from here and there's a boat leaving today. My sister Teré lives on the island. She'll fix you up with a place.'

Dad frowned. He looked terribly disappointed.

'But Aitutaki is not a desert island. I need a desert island, William.'

'Wait a moment, Tony, and I'll tell you. Aitutaki has a beautiful lagoon. On this lagoon is a *motu* called Maina. That should be just what you require. It's a very small *motu*, three and a half miles from the main island. You can go and live there! Then your newspaper men will come and take their photographs and, after the waiting time is finished, you can get on the boat from Aitutaki to Palmerston. After that, go to Primrose *motu*, as John James Marsters said you could. Why not?'

Dad looked at Mum and she shrugged. It looked as if they had no choice.

'Is Maina really uninhabited?' Dad asked.

'Except for the crabs and maybe a few chickens. You will be glad of those, eh, kids?'

He looked round at Stacey, Craig and Matthew, his eyes crinkling so much as he smiled that they almost closed. Matthew was enthusiastic. He remembered William ringing his chicken bell the day before.

'Can we train them to come when we call, like you did?'

'Of course, no problem. You just need patience and a bit of understanding.'

'Let's go there, then,' said Matthew.

And so, with no further hanging around, it was fixed.

Back at his house, William Richards phoned his sister Teré and explained the situation. Teré said she would meet the boat.

'Very good,' said William, returning from the telephone, rubbing his hands with pleasure at the arrangements he had made. 'The boat leaves this afternoon. But first you must have a good meal with us, to celebrate. A traditional island meal, cooked in our special way.'

The special way was by means of a sunken oven. First a number of volcanic rocks were heated on a fire until they were too hot to touch. They were then rolled into the bottom of a rectangular pit, which had been dug in the ground near the house and lined with sheets of steel or iron. On top of the hot rocks a wire tray was placed, containing chickens, papaw, breadfruit, sweet potatoes and other produce, before the whole thing was covered by a metal lid. The volcanic rocks, said William, would hold their heat so well that, when the lid was removed in a couple of hours, everything would be slow-roasted to perfection.

And so it was. The chickens went in all white, pimpled and naked-looking. But they came out golden roasted and every bit as succulent as William had prophesied. Stacey watched the whole process wide-eyed, deeply impressed.

'Is this why these are called the Cook Islands?' she asked Mary, taking her hand and swinging from it.

It was a great meal. But after they had eaten came the farewells at the quayside, and hugs all round. After only two days on Rarotonga, Craig, Matthew and Stacey felt they had been taken into this large, seemingly chaotic family of William Richards. They felt they had been made a part of it and they were all, in some way, sorry to be saying goodbye.

'Come and see us when you come back,' said Mary, kissing them all one by one. 'We'll have another feast.'

'Yes,' said William, turning to Mum and Dad. 'If you like, you can go back to England and leave the kids with us. I'll adopt them as part of my family until you return. Then you can come back to us later after your book is published.'

They all laughed at the idea, but Mum said later that she wasn't sure if he was really joking or not.

'I do think he really would adopt you, if he got the chance,' she said. 'What do *you* think of the idea?'

'What does adopt mean?' asked Stacey.

'It means William would become your dad instead of me,' said Dad.

'Oh no,' said Stacey, shaking her pigtails. 'He can't be my dad. He can be my Bampa if he likes.'

'You've already got one Bampa,' pointed out Mum.

'I can have *two* Bampas, can't I?' said Stacey firmly.

As their ship drew away from the jetty and made its way through the narrow gap in the reef, a small, white, brand-new-looking aircraft rose into the air from Rarotonga's airport behind them. Its twin engines cut through the blue atmosphere with a crude, incongruous scream, like your next-door neighbour's lawnmower churning into a tangle of rusty wire. But, however much it set everybody's teeth on edge, the plane was a sign of altering times.

When island-hopping by air becomes normal, novelty and change will spread like brushfire through the Cook Islands. For a hundred years of colonialism, and another hundred of occasional visits by European seafarers before that, the way of life had been affected only slowly. True, there have been many Cook Islanders migrating to find work, so that today there are more islanders in New Zealand than at home. But the way of life of those remaining has (so far) been in good enough shape to blend with European ideas, mostly because change was always slow. The first hospital was not founded in Rarotonga until the 1950s. Package tourists didn't begin to arrive until the 1970s, and even today they only come in small groups. Some islands had no electricity until 1985 and the third largest of them – Atiu – still has power for only twelve hours a day.

But landing-strips are gradually being built on all of the northern atolls, which lie furthest from Rarotonga – one is even planned, William Richards had said, on Palmerston, with its population of only fifty. Dad thought these developments were not good news. The islanders' present style of life would hardly survive the shocks: mass package-tourism, hotel chains, high-speed power boats, satellite television, a 'consumer boom'. On Rarotonga, they were already mixing the concrete for a big Sheraton Hotel. It was another sign of the times, and the islanders would have to adapt to them or die.

'They changed quickly before,' Dad told Craig, 'when they had to. The first time the Papa'a, as the Europeans were known, came to these islands, two hundred and fifty years ago, they brought dysentery and measles with them. The islanders had never had these sicknesses, of course, and many, many of them were killed. The people had to throw the dead bodies into lime-pits, because there weren't enough healthy people left to bury them and say prayers over them.'

The prayers they would have liked to say weren't Christian prayers, Dad said. Not at first. The gods of the original islanders were many: a shark god, a wave god, a sun god, a hurricane god – seventy-one gods altogether. But when the Papa'a missionaries came, they set about wiping out the old religions, destroying all the carvings of the gods wherever they found them.

'They also stopped the islanders eating human flesh,' he told them.

Craig and Matthew were naturally interested in cannibalism, and had already asked William Richards about it. Yes, William had told them, the ancestors of the islanders *had* once eaten people. But not for food.

'They believed in a power called *mana*. It's a sort of magic influence by one person over another person. A man with *mana* could make another fellow grow rich or poor, sick or well. He could even make him die, if he was very powerful. And it was because of *mana* that they would be cannibals, sometimes. You see, they believed if you ate the flesh of a man who had much *mana*, you could take over all of that power and keep it for yourself. So it was a kind of a ritual more than a meal; a bit of magic.'

'Did they eat sailors who came from Britain?' Matthew wanted to know.

William laughed. 'Why d'you think they call them Papa'a? They saw a ship coming and they rubbed their tummies and said, "Papa! Ahhh!"'

It was an old joke. But in reality, it would be closer to the truth to say the islanders were 'eaten' by the Europeans. And the islanders didn't really fight back, because they could see for themselves all the wealth and the many

44

useful machines and gadgets which the Europeans owned. So when the missionaries started to tell them that these good things had a lot to do with the teachings of Jesus Christ, the island people became convinced. Then they agreed to give up their old gods and become Christians.

They still believe a lot of the old things, of course, even now. They believe in Christianity too, but they also hold that the spirits of their ancestors live on in the islands with them. And they still believe in the power of *mana* – but not cannibalism.

Leaning like a pair of seasoned mariners on the ship's rail, Craig and Matthew looked back at the peak of Rarotonga's deep-sleeping volcano, with its lush pelt of vegetation. It was the first South Sea island they had known, and they already loved it. The desert island, they now supposed, would be a version of the same thing, miniaturized of course. But, in thinking this, they were wrong. Over the next few months Craig, Matthew and Stacey would come to know, not one, but two uninhabited *motus* and they would turn out to be very different from the massively imposing emerald cone that was gradually shrinking away from them.

It was an uncomfortable, queasy night, with the little ship slipping and sliding around in a liquid mountain-range, like a toy. There were cabins, but they spent most of the hours of darkness on deck, breathing the fresh air, talking a little, sleeping fitfully. Dad, not a good sailor, thought of the miles of ocean water which lay beneath their keel. He couldn't even swim. If the boat should turn over . . .

At last morning came and they watched Aitutaki

stealing up over the northern horizon. It too had a volcanic mountain, but it was only one-fifth as high as the peak which dominates Raro – more of a hump, really. On the map, Aitutaki Island is shaped like a Cook Islands fish hook: the wide part of it – the shaft of the hook – lies north–south and curling round from the top, like a dog's hind leg, is a narrow strip of land. Here sits an airstrip built by the US Air Force during the Second World War.

The roughly triangular reef which frames Aitutaki's lagoon has sides, each about seven miles long. Dotted around the perimeter, just visible inside the reef, several *motus* could be seen with Maina, their own island, amongst them. As the ship's captain throttled back his engines before making a cautious passage through the reef, they scanned these low, sandy islets sprouting with coconut palms and wondered which one of them was Maina. From this distance, all the *motus* looked disappointingly like bumps of sand in the sea. Matthew looked over the ship's side, into the glassy water. He could see the small, vivid fish – orange, blue, green, spotted, candy-striped – jetting around like maniacs. He wondered how they would taste after Mum had cooked some of them.

Waiting to greet them on the jetty was Teré, the sister of William Richards. She was a grey-haired woman, with a voice to match her large size. Behind her a blue minibus was waiting.

'Welcome to Aitutaki,' she boomed, even before they had come ashore. Then, with their luggage stacked on the dockside, she shook hands with Mum and Dad and beamed at the children.

'You're coming to my house to eat. Later we'll take

you over to Maina in our boat. Come on. Let's get these bags into the bus.'

Teré was strong. She hoisted the two suitcases so easily they might have been empty. In fact they were stuffed with clothes, equipment and stores, including the tent and sleeping-bags. With the bags stowed in the back of the minibus, they were off to Teré's house.

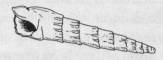

8

Maina

Waiting for them was Palmer Marsters, the younger brother of William Richards and Teré. He looked just like them, as if he'd come out of the same jelly-mould only slightly more recently. He was maybe ten years younger than his sister. After he'd greeted them he gave a bronchial cough and tapped his hand against his broad chest, smiling sadly.

'I've caught the flu, I think. So I'm not taking you over to Maina.'

Mum and Dad looked alarmed. Oh no, not another delay, they were thinking. Palmer waved his hand in the air.

'Don't worry, you're still going today. My sister can sail the boat. You'll take them, won't you, Teré?'

'Of course. Absolutely no problem,' Teré insisted. 'But we'll have to leave right after we've eaten. The sun round here sets early, about four o'clock, and I want to get back before dark. You can't use a boat around the lagoon at night, because of the reefs. You'd be getting shipwrecked all the time.'

Inside the house they met Teré's aged father, Richard Marsters, one of the many grandsons of the first, legendary William Marsters of Palmerston. Richard had been a Christian missionary all his life, preaching first on the island of Atiu before coming to Aitutaki. He had, he told them, built this house, and another one next door to it, with his own hands.

'Jesus was a carpenter, you know,' he laughed. 'It's a most respectable profession.'

They looked around the house. The craftsmanship was very good. Matthew marvelled at the polished turtle-shells, as big as wash-basins, which hung on the walls instead of pictures.

Meanwhile, Craig was showing his electronic game, Bank Raid, to Junior Marsters, Teré's seventeen-year-old grandson. Junior was fascinated by the way you could move the little figures around the screen by manipulating a pair of buttons. It was like a gripping story to him: he couldn't put it down.

They hadn't been at Teré's house more than half an hour when everyone sat down for a huge meal. Craig, Matthew and Stacey, having got over their seasickness, were starving. They thought they'd never tasted anything as wonderful as the fish, breadfruit and baked green bananas.

'Do you need anything for your stores, Tony?' Palmer asked as they ate. 'Maybe I can let you have a few things.'

Dad was touched. He didn't want to accept too much help, because his plan was to make the island as much like a shipwreck as possible. They would live off the land and the sea only, as he'd made clear back in Wales. But there was one vital thing he lacked.

'I don't have a fishing-net, Palmer. I was going to buy one, but . . .

'You haven't got a net? That's no problem. I can let you have one.'

49

Palmer went out of the room and returned with a small-mesh net, folded up. He tossed it to Dad. With it were some fishing-hooks, wrapped in paper.

'What else do you want? I'll give you a tin container for fresh water – you can take it full and then, when it's empty, you use it to collect the rain.' Then, as an afterthought, he asked, 'You've got a machete, haven't you?'

Dad looked shocked. He shook his head. They should have got one on Rarotonga, but he'd completely forgotten. Palmer made no remark. He just coughed and wandered into the house, patting his chest. He came back a few minutes later with a simple metre-long machete, which he handed to Dad.

'Take it. You wouldn't last long without the net and this little tool. They're basic equipment, as you know.'

'Thanks, Palmer,' said Dad, laughing. 'You might have saved our lives.'

Palmer's boat, four and a half metres long, powered by an outboard motor, lay pulled up high on the beach. Under her keel was a series of wooden poles which acted as rollers for launching her into the water. Mum, Dad, Teré and Junior heaved, while the children moved the rollers from one end to the other, and they soon had the boat bobbing in the surf. They loaded the cases, rucksacks, water and fishing gear. With a broad smile, Teré produced a gift of her own: a sack of melons which she tucked in under one of the thwarts.

'These are the best fruit when you're thirsty. Even better than green coconuts.'

Then they boarded the boat one by one, with Junior and Craig pushing her out beyond the breakers until there was enough water to lower the propeller. As the two boys jumped aboard, Teré gave a strong pull on the starting cord and the carburettor gave a few splutters and coughs. Then, with a strong smell of exhaust, the engine fired and roared.

Fully loaded, with the stores as well as human cargo, she was riding low in the water and progress was sluggish.

'We couldn't have done this at all yesterday,' said Teré, steering straight out into the lagoon. 'This is the hurricane season, you know. It began to blow hard, really blow, the waves dashing through the reef and rough water even inside the lagoon. The waves reached, oh, twenty metres up the beach. But –' She smiled and shrugged. 'When we woke up this morning, it was bright sunshine again. No hurricane.'

It was certainly a calm, beautiful day. Teré had put up a huge, colourful umbrella to shade her from the rays. Dad, on the other hand, pulled off his T-shirt, thinking he would sunbathe. But when she saw him Teré shouted, sounding almost angry.

'Tony! Put your shirt back on at once! You get terrible sunburn out here, you know that? I've seen tourists nearly die from it.'

Sheepishly, Dad covered himself again. If Teré gave orders, it was clear they were to be obeyed. She was that kind of person.

As they reached deeper water, Matthew was hanging over the side, peering down to see what was happening in the clear water-world below. Beside him, Junior was holding a loaded spear gun. He nudged Matthew's arm.

'Look, there. Swordfish.'

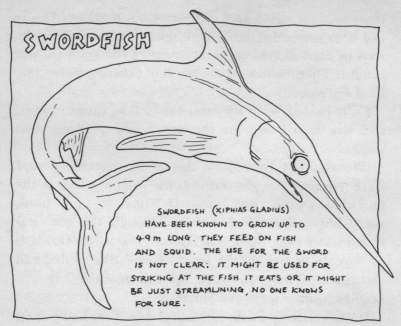

SWORDFISH

SWORDFISH (XIPHIAS GLADIUS)
HAVE BEEN KNOWN TO GROW UP TO
4.9 m LONG. THEY FEED ON FISH
AND SQUID. THE USE FOR THE SWORD
IS NOT CLEAR; IT MIGHT BE USED FOR
STRIKING AT THE FISH IT EATS OR IT MIGHT
BE JUST STREAMLINING, NO ONE KNOWS
FOR SURE.

Straight away, Matthew saw it – a long, streamlined, silver torpedo racing alongside the boat. He pushed his face lower, fascinated. He was almost eyeball to eyeball with it. Junior touched his shoulder, pulling him back out of the way. Then he aimed his spear gun and fired, the line whipping out behind the spear like a cobra striking at its prey. But the shot missed and the fish sheered off to safety.

Junior said something in Maori, then added, 'Pity I missed. The fish would make a good dinner for you on Maina.'

His mention of the island made Matthew and Craig look up, squinting towards the horizon. Then suddenly Dad pointed.

'Craig! Matthew! Do you see it? Over there.'

They were heading directly into the sun. The boys

shaded their eyes. They could see the shallow hump of an island, sandy at the base, lush green vegetation around the top, and the whole crowned with tall coconut palms. In a horizontal line extending from each tip of the *motu* was the foaming thread of reef: the lagoon's boundary.

'That's it!' Dad shouted. 'That's Maina!'

They went ashore straight on to the beach. Maina was an island in a completely natural state – there was no jetty or landing-stage or mooring of any kind.

'There's no point in building anything here,' Teré told them. 'If anything was built it would be smashed up by the wind next time there was a hurricane. Anyway, these *motus* are always changing shape. The wind blows the trees away and then the sand shifts around.'

Dad and the boys unshipped stores while Teré walked Mum up the beach, pointing out places to make camp. Stacey was tearing up and down the surf, jumping over waves and shouting with glee. When the women returned, Teré was looking at her watch and the sun. It was already declining towards the horizon. She pushed a strand of grey hair away from her face.

'Look, we've got to get going. Will you be OK?'

Craig noticed a look on her face, just a passing expression of concern. He thought, She's wondering if she's doing the right thing, leaving us here.

'Don't worry, Teré,' said Dad, putting on his most charming smile. 'We're as right as rain here.'

At that, Teré laughed. 'I tell you, you won't get much rain – except when you get *too* much. Be careful.'

Teré climbed into the boat and Junior walked it into deeper water. At the last minute, Craig dug into the pocket of his rucksack and pulled out Bank Raid. It would feel pretty silly playing it out here, in the wilderness. And sooner or later the batteries would run out. He splashed out towards the boat and handed it to Junior.

'Here,' he said. 'A present.'

Junior's surprise and delight were reward in themselves. He tucked the game into the pocket of his shorts. Then Teré lowered the outboard, pulled the cord and it belched into life.

'Goodbye,' shouted Teré as Craig waded back to the beach. When he got there the boat was already a hundred metres out and picking up speed. Changing direction slightly, Teré set a course for Aitutaki, which they now realized was clearly visible in the distance. They could see Junior waving his arm in a wide semicircle. They waved back. Teré cupped her hand around her mouth.

'See you again when we bring the men from London. Take care.'

'We will,' shouted Dad. 'Bye.'

They watched as the little boat shrank and shrank. The turquoise water was a shade darker as the afternoon light grew less intense, and it was getting harder to make out the shape of the boat. But even before they finally lost sight of it, the sound of the outboard had faded to nothing against the churning surf.

'What did she mean?' said Matthew to his brother. 'About not getting much rain except when we get too much?'

'She's talking about storms, stupid,' said Craig. 'Hurricanes.'

'Touch wood,' ordered Mum quickly. 'We don't want one of those, do we?'

Craig quickly looked around the sand. There was no wood to touch.

'Well, if we want to make a fire, we'd better go and gather some,' said Dad.

9

Halfway to Paradise

They set out at once to survey the island, which, they found, was not much more than three hundred metres long, with two basic types of terrain. The interior consisted of fairly poor-quality soil in which a scrub of green vegetation grew, most of it low bushes. Only the pipe-cleaner trunks of the coconut palms reached any height, as the splay of their fronds waved in the breeze resembling giant bunches of green feathers. Around the island, like the brim of a hat, was a wide, flat beach. It had the purest white sand the children had ever seen.

Looking for shade, Mum found a spot to pitch camp. It was behind a banian-tree just above the top of the beach. They drew the tent out of its sausage-shaped bag, unrolled it, and in ten minutes it was up, a barrel-tent in orange nylon, supported by metal hoops and guy-ropes. Then, while Mum set about making a fire, Dad called Craig.

'Come on, we've got to go and fish for our supper.'

They took Palmer's fishing-net and walked along the beach to a quiet spot, where Dad said there would be plenty of unsuspecting fish.

'No one's been on here for a long time, I reckon. The fish will probably swim into the net like they're going to a birthday party.'

Craig stood on the beach holding one end of the net,

which was shaped like a tennis net, except that it had a much smaller mesh and had cork floats attached around the edge. Holding his end of the net by its corners, Dad waded seven or eight metres into the water, paying out the net behind him. The fish darted and played around his legs. They seemed to have no fear.

'OK. Now I lower the net into the water like so, and then pull it round.'

Still holding the corners of the net apart, but with most of it now submerged, Dad drew it through the water in a short semicircle. He took just a few steps, before putting the corners of the net together again and wading back to join Craig. They hauled in the net and examined their catch. Scores of fish were struggling in the tight mesh: grey, silver and gold fish, and a lot of multi-coloured individuals – reds, blues and yellows. There was none larger than the size of a sprat or a sardine.

'Yes,' said Dad, 'they're small. But I think we've got enough here for our supper.'

And that was fishing. You might have said it was easy as pie, except that, there on Maina, a pie would have been rather a difficult proposition. Fishing, however, took less effort than picking the blackberries for a pie back home.

'Let's go and see if Mum's got that fire going,' said Dad.

So they gathered up the net and carried it, still containing its catch, back to the camp. Mum had made a fireplace, and they sat down beside it to pick out the fish that they would eat for supper. Most had to be grasped around the gills and pulled sharply to release them from the net, because their fins had become entangled. Dad showed which fish they could safely eat – which basically meant the boring ones. All the vivid, tropical-type fish were taken back to the water and released.

The camp faced west, straight into the orange glow of the setting sun. Aitutaki was out of sight behind them, over the hump of the interior.

'It's better this way,' said Dad with a sigh, popping a raw tiddler into his mouth. 'Ideally, I would prefer it if Aitutaki was over the horizon. Still, at least you can't see anything from here except the reef and the Pacific Ocean.'

He crunched the fish and swallowed contentedly. He felt he had made it. He was here, in Paradise.

But there were drawbacks to Paradise, very serious drawbacks, and the children were unprepared for them. The first, and worst, was sunburn.

No one had felt like taking Teré's warnings seriously and, within a couple of days, the whole family was severely burnt. Here, in the southern hemisphere, sunshine is literally blistering, and will probably become worse as the aerosol sprays and refrigeration plants of civilization go on releasing quantities of chlorofluorocarbon gases, or CFCs, into the atmosphere. These gases do no direct harm to us, but when they rise above a height of around twenty kilometres, CFCs begin to attack the thick layer of ozone which cocoons the earth and soaks up the most harmful of the sun's non-visible rays. Where the ozone layer is attacked, it becomes thinner and so lets more harmful rays reach the earth. And, the more harmful the rays which get to us in sunlight, the more horribly sunburnt we can become.

This just goes to show how hard it can be to escape the influence of civilization – however far you travel on this planet.

The children had been sunburnt before, of course. There had been hot summers when perhaps they'd spent a little too long on Mumbles Beach, so that their skin grew red and felt a little sore. But after a few hours it would right itself and turn gradually into a tan. But this was a different matter. In fact, it was grotesque, as if they'd been singed by the fire of a furnace or an explosion. The outer layer of skin, especially on their shoulders and faces, lifted off in blisters. Beneath these suppurating bubbles, the living skin was hot, and tender as raw meat. It also smelt – first burnt and then putrid.

Matters were made much worse, in those first few days, by the need to sleep in the tent. Night-time on Maina was oppressively hot and swarming with voracious mosquitoes and other biting flies. But they had packed no mosquito nets and so, to avoid being the insects' dinner, they were forced to zip up inside their tent. And soon Dad was cursing his lack of foresight in bringing this piece of equipment. The tent was absolutely fine for camping halfway up an Alpine mountain or in the Brecon Beacons, but not in the South Seas. The atmosphere inside the closed tent was choking, sweaty and – thanks to the sunburn sores – evil-smelling.

Then there was The Sound. It was Stacey who heard it first, one evening, after dark, when she was sitting at the entrance to the tent, getting ready for sleep. Dad was off somewhere along the beach. Mum was sitting by the fire, holding a pan over the flames. Her brothers were hunting crabs by torchlight.

It had come from somewhere in the interior, but quite close. It was a weird sound, a mewling or a sobbing, high-pitched and sorrowful. And yet Stacey had heard something like it before. The Sound stopped and Stacey thought back. What did it remind her of? At first she couldn't think. She waited until she heard it again. There it was, echoing through the undergrowth. It seemed to be just the other side of the tent. She put her hands against her face, eyes wide open in fear. She knew what it sounded like now. A baby. An *abandoned* baby, crying and crying for her mother.

At first Stacey just sat there, rigid from fear. Then cautiously she looked around her. Everything was pitch dark. She could just make out Mum's face reflected in the fireglow.

'Mum! Mum!'

Mum looked towards her.

'What is it, Stacey?'

'Mum, there's a baby crying behind the tent.'

Mum listened. There was nothing to hear, not now. The Sound had stopped.

'There's nothing, Stacey. Come on, into bed. Get some sleep.'

Stacey lay alone in the tent. She could hear Craig and Matthew messing about somewhere on the beach, playing by torchlight. Then she heard Dad call out.

'Hey, boys. Put out that torch! Don't waste the battery.'

Then they had only the moonlight to play by. The night went quiet. Stacey heard someone moving around outside the tent; she heard a scraping sound and a bush rustling. And then, suddenly, The Sound came again. Stacey couldn't help herself. She screamed.

Mum heard and came into the tent to lie beside her. Stacey was snuffling gently to herself.

'What's the matter, Stace? What're you crying for?'

'Mum, it's not me crying. It's the baby. I don't like that baby crying. I don't like the baby crying.'

'Don't worry, your mummy's here. Don't you worry now.'

So Mum cuddled her and she began to feel better. Then Dad called from outside the tent.

'What's the matter, Cath?'

'Stacey's hearing things. Says she can hear a baby crying.'

At last Stacey dropped off to sleep. A little later, Dad heard it too: a thin, miserable sobbing. Then a large bird got up from the undergrowth and flapped away across the interior. Mina birds, with their gift for imitation, are common in the Cook Islands. Dad told Mum he'd solved the mystery of the crying baby.

It was morning and Matthew was off in the interior. He had his men with him, the figures he'd bought with his injection money. The interior of the island made a fine background for playing with the men, a tropical jungle in which he could imagine all kinds of Indiana Jones adventures and missions. Matthew preferred to play with the men alone, because that way he could use his own imagination to make up any rules he wanted. Craig sometimes played, but he always wanted to make the rules up himself, and that wasn't the same thing at all. Anyway, Craig was crazy about swimming. Matthew thought he could hear him now, splashing about in the lagoon like a dolphin. Craig was a good swimmer,

61

unlike Matthew. All in all, he preferred his men.

He found a place where a palm tree had fallen down. He put his two Terminator figures on the horizontal trunk and started to make them crawl along its length, keeping their heads down to avoid enemy fire coming from ahead. He was so busy making the sounds of rapid automatic fire that he wasn't sure what that other noise he'd heard might be. He stopped playing for a moment and listened.

Chooorrk-chook-chook – chooorrk-chook-chook-chook.

It was coming from the ground on the other side of a clump of bushes. He went to investigate and, to his amazement, found himself face to face with a little, brown, farmyard hen, pecking the dust. She stopped what she was doing and stood up, looking at him, her head inclined as if to say, 'Goodness gracious! Matthew Ryan Williams. Fancy meeting *you* here!'

Matthew pushed cautiously past the hen. There was a small clearing, with a brood of six yellow chicks milling

around in the middle of it. As soon as Matthew went near them the mother came up at the run, making her mother hen's anxious droodling sound. She rounded the brood up and shooed them nervously into the undergrowth.

Matthew ran back and reported his find to Dad.

'Good,' he said. 'One night, we can have chicken for our dinner.'

On their first trip, Dad and Mum had been taught by their friend Kuraka-Kuraka how to kill and eat a wild chicken, and they were determined to try it. A trap was set up using the fishing-net, and soon one of the adult birds strolled into it, pecking up a trail of coconut chips. Craig dropped the net and they pounced. The hen was their prisoner.

Craig, Matthew and Stacey looked at Dad, wondering what he was going to do now. Mum couldn't watch. She took Stacey away to the other end of the island. Steeling himself, Dad grasped the bird's neck through the net mesh and started wringing it, like a wet dishcloth. Matthew turned his head away.

When the bird was dead, it had to be plucked and its guts taken out. Dad used his gutting knife. It was a messy, bloody job, but at last it was done. The bird looked *something* like the chicken they were used to seeing Mum put in the oven for Sunday lunch, though it would never have been acceptable on Tesco's poultry counter. It was scrawny and stringy and, when Mum roasted it over the fire, it tasted of earth. They tried the experiment twice more, but only Stacey could honestly say she liked it.

Eventually, they took a census of all the chickens and gave them names. The mother hen was called Meg while the cock was King. There was also a second, younger male who naturally became known as Prince. Tubs was a fat little chick; Teenager was larger and cheekier than the rest, while poor Lucky was the runt of the brood – always staggering along behind the rest of her family and never getting enough to eat. Mum became particularly attached to Lucky. She would catch her and give her special meals, stroking and tickling the back of her neck. One day Mum noticed that Lucky had a weepy, possibly infected eye. With warm, salty water, Mum tried to bathe the affected eye, while the tiny bird struggled and cheeped like a telephone.

Stacey used to feed the hens by tossing small chunks of coconut on the ground, forcing the wary Meg to come almost (but not quite) near enough to be touched. Stacey loved the way the mother hen used to field the scraps of coconut in her beak, break them into smaller pieces and toss them to her chicks, who would squabble fiercely over them. Suddenly Stacey had a memory of her school, back in Swansea. When they came here, Stacey had completed only her first term, but she remembered it all perfectly. This milling crowd of little cheepers looked just like some aeroplane's view of the Infants' playground, with the children scrambling over each other, playing kiss chase and tug of war.

Gradually they all became fond of the chickens and, of course, once they had christened them, they couldn't eat them any more. And there was a little part in all of them which was ashamed of the chickens they had eaten. Looking back, it even felt a little like cannibalism.

10

Hurricane force

By the time they'd been seven days on Maina, the worst effects of sunburn began to ease, and already the mosquito bites seemed less itchy. Their accommodation, though it would never be the Ritz, had become a little more comfortable. With Craig and Matthew, Dad had built a shelter above the beach, two hundred metres from the camp. The frame was constructed out of driftwood and fallen branches and this they thatched with palm fronds. It was a rough and ready affair, but at least it gave shade while the children did their schoolwork or dozed through the afternoon heat.

The weather continued searingly hot. Craig spent most of the time paddling himself around the shallows on his back, watching the terns squabbling over fish, and the vicious piratical behaviour of the frigate-birds. These large, hook-billed bullies never bothered to catch food for themselves, but lived by stealing it from the terns. They would glide around, torpidly riding the thermal air-currents, until they saw a tern rising up from the sea with a particularly tasty morsel. Then, looping craftily down to the same altitude, the frigate-bird would start to menace the smaller bird, flying around it and squawking, until the victim was forced into a self-defensive peck at the harasser. But this, of course, meant she had to open her beak, releasing the catch. With a sudden flash of

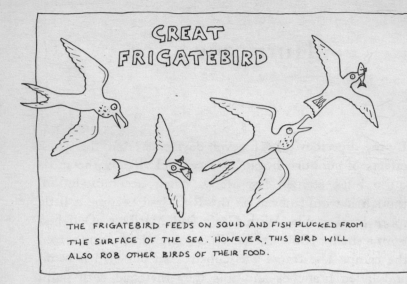

GREAT FRIGATEBIRD

THE FRIGATEBIRD FEEDS ON SQUID AND FISH PLUCKED FROM THE SURFACE OF THE SEA. HOWEVER, THIS BIRD WILL ALSO ROB OTHER BIRDS OF THEIR FOOD.

unexpected energy, the frigate would swoop down and neatly trap the plummeting fish in its own beak, before flying away as he greedily gobbled it down.

But these days of lazing around, beach-combing, swimming, spoiling the chickens, were about to come to an end. It happened in a way which they *should* have been prepared for. They were not.

They sensed the change from the moment of waking up. Something was different. The air was unusually quiet, the birds silent and the chickens had disappeared. When Craig climbed a palm tree to collect the day's supply of coconuts, the line of surf which marked the reef was clearly whiter and more turbulent than he had seen before. Out beyond the reef, the vast ocean had always heaved with tremendous waves. Now they were rolling

FOR THIS PIRACY THE FRIGATEBIRD
HAS EARNED ITSELF THE ALTERNATIVE
NAMES OF THE SEA HAWK AND THE MAN OF WAR.

in and smashing against the reef with pulverizing force. On the normally placid lagoon, the first anxious ripples began to appear.

'Change in the weather,' said Dad. He had been through the interior to look at the sky and water on the other side. 'Clouds are massing in the east. We'll lose the sun next.'

Within half an hour, the sun had gone. It was humid, sticky, and even though a breeze had begun to get up, it came in hot uncomfortable gusts. By mid-morning the lagoon had developed choppy wavelets, with those flag-like shiny crests known as white horses leaping out and disappearing in a random pattern all the way from Maina to Aitutaki.

Everyone shared the sense of unease. And, while they carried out the usual tasks – fishing, adding more thatch to the shelter, schoolwork, husking coconuts – they were done fretfully and without heart. The wind picked up all through the afternoon until, at dusk, the lagoon was running a sea of two-metre waves, which rolled in and crashed violently on to the beach. In normal times the tide's edge was between fifteen and twenty metres below the camp. But now these breakers had started surging up the sand to within ten, and then five metres.

Dad kept saying, 'Don't worry, Cath. It'll die away in the night. We'll be all right, this is a good strong tent.'

But both of them knew that they were still in the hurricane season, and that their tent wasn't built to withstand the terrifying violence of a South Seas storm at full blast. But where else could they go? The tent was certainly stronger than Dad's shelter, which, as the wind tugged and pushed it, was beginning to look increasingly flimsy.

So, when the rain began, the children were ordered into their sleeping-bags. Dad and Mum took a last look at the raging sea before joining them, optimistically zipping up the tent flap.

'What's happening?' asked Craig.

'Wind's still getting stronger,' said Dad.

As if to confirm this, there came a sharp crack, clearly heard over the roar of the storm, as a nearby tree broke under the strain. It was followed by a disturbance around the tent, some thuds and an object falling against the nylon flysheet, which sagged under the weight. Dad looked out then pulled back his head.

'The shelter's gone. Just collapsed like a house of cards. Part of it's on top of the tent.'

He meant the play-hut which Craig had built for Stacey, beside the tent.

Mum said, 'Look, we can't stay here. We're under the trees. If one of them comes down on us we'll be crushed.'

Dad hesitated for a moment. A gust of wind seemed to slip a huge hand underneath the tent and try to lift it, tugging hard. Dad made up his mind.

'You're right,' he said. 'We've got to move out.'

He ripped the flap fastener open and rolled out into the wind. The highest waves were only a metre away now, lashing at the roots of the banian tree. He started uprooting the skewers which held the tent guy-ropes in place, while Mum pushed the children outside and started cramming things at random into suitcases and rucksacks.

'Where shall we go?' she yelled.

'We need open ground, but we've got to get off the beach. These waves are still getting bigger. We'll be washed away if we stay on the shore.'

'We can go to the clearing,' said Craig.

'Yes, that's the best place. Come on.'

The clearing was a patch of ground to the north of the camp in which there were no significant trees or bushes. It was the obvious place to avoid falling palm trees.

The wind seemed like something solid. Craig stood up and was immediately thrown to the ground by the force of it. The rain lashed his face and hair. It was pitch dark. Somewhere nearby a flying coconut crashed into the sand.

'Where's the torch?' Dad was shouting. Mum found it in the tent and gave it to Craig.

'Boys, take your rucksacks.' Dad was yelling to be heard above the wind and waves. 'You light the way, Craig. I'm carrying Stacey.'

'I can't even walk, Dad. The wind's too strong.'

'Then crawl.'

They waited while Dad pulled the tent right down, flattening it and laying the fallen remnants of the shelter on top, in the hope of anchoring it down. Then, crouching low, sometimes being knocked on to hands and knees by the wind, Matthew and Craig started along the upper edge of the beach. Mum followed, dragging one of the suitcases behind her, while Dad brought up the rear. He had the second case in one hand and Stacey in the other.

'I'll come back for the tent,' he shouted. 'Keep moving.'

There was a path which led from the beach to the clearing, about seventy-five metres away. It seemed like a mile. As they fought their way to it, towering waves pounded the beach with such force that they could feel the shock waves under their feet. The water surged ferociously up the slope to soak their ankles. Flying, salty foam mixed with the rain that was lashing their faces. Matthew felt that at any moment the wind could take him off his feet, spin him up in the air and send him flying over the ocean like a piece of scrap paper. He had never seen anything like the frenzy of the sea.

At last they reached the clearing. The trees around the edge were bending at an angle of forty-five degrees. Across the clearing airborne coconuts, broken branches and debris of all kinds were flying uncontrollably. Stacey's face was rigid with fear, her eyes as big as Cook Islands dollar coins. Dad lowered her to her feet.

For a moment Stacey stood beside her father, grasping him around the thigh. Then, with almost casual strength, the wind plucked her off her feet, and she went tumbling and somersaulting away from him. He ran and caught her up again. She was screaming. Dad calmed her down and asked if she was hurt. Stacey shook her head.

Dad looked wildly around. There was a palm tree which stood near the edge of the bushes, but a little apart from them. It seemed more solid than the others, and was bending less. Dad ran Stacey across to this tree and put her down beside it. Holding her with her back to the tree-trunk, he unwound a length of guy-rope from his waist. He started to wrap it round Stacey's body and around the trunk of the tree.

Mum shouted, 'Tony! What are you doing?'

'Frisbie did this on Suwarrow. Tied his children to the trees. That was how they survived. We could all be washed away if there's a tidal wave.'

Frisbie was an American writer who had lived with his family during the Second World War on the deserted atoll of Suwarrow, in the northern group of the Cook Islands, and described how he had bound his family to coconut palms to stop them blowing away when a hurricane struck. Perhaps he had got the idea from an old film from the 1930s, *Hurricane*, in which the heroine was lashed to a palm tree by the hero to prevent her being swept into the sea.

Mum ran over and bent to look into Stacey's face. She was struggling with Dad, trying to squirm away from him.

'No!' she screamed. 'I don't want to be tied up. No! No! No!'

But Dad persisted, trying to hold her still. Suddenly she went still, holding herself rigidly. Mum hammered Dad on the arm.

'Tony, she's holding her breath. She's hysterical.'

Dad stopped what he was doing and, with Craig shining the torch, he examined Stacey's face. By now it had started to turn red. Soon it would be purple.

'Tony, let her go. Free her!'

Reluctantly, Dad began to unwind the rope. Soon Stacey was released and breathing again, clasped in Mum's arms. Together they sank to the ground. Dad started back towards the beach, shouting to them, 'I'll go and get the tent.'

He returned ten minutes later, dragging the tent behind him like the empty skin of an animal. The rain was still lashing. He dumped the tent down.

'Come on, everybody get inside. It's no use putting it up.'

They crawled into the tent, dragging the cases and rucksacks behind them, and settled down in the dark to sit out the storm. The collapsed tent lay on top of them. They were damp and shivering with cold.

Craig remembered stories Dad had told him about hurricanes, and the tremendous force of sea and wind they could generate. There had been another volunteer castaway, Tom Neale, who succeeded Frisbie on Suwarrow. Neale had repaired the island's seventy-metre-long jetty, which was destroyed in Frisbie's 1942 hurricane. With his bare hands, he had trundled each of the massive blocks of coral rock (the basis of the original jetty's piers or stanchions) back into position from the beach, where the hurricane had hurled them. It took

Our house in
West Cross,
Swansea
(*Daily Mirror*)

Outside school
in Wales . . .
(*Daily Mirror*)

. . . and school outside on a desert island
(*Daily Mirror*)

Stacey drinking
from a coconut
(*Daily Mirror*)

In the shade of
our tent
(*Daily Mirror*)

Stacey catching
up on some
sleep after the
storm
(*Daily Mirror*)

Gathering palm leaves to make a hut and give us some shade
(*Daily Mirror*)

Fishing desert-island style
(*Daily Mirror*)

The canoe we used to leave our island
(*Daily Mirror*)

Craig, Stacey and Matthew
surrounded by palm leaves
(*Daily Mirror*)

him months of back-breaking labour before he finished the job.

But Neale had no time to savour his success. Only twenty-four hours after he'd finished the job, as if from pure spite, a new hurricane struck the atoll. The storm raged all day and, when it was exhausted, Neale found that it had flung the entire jetty back in his face. It tore away the deck boards and demolished the framework. Then, uprooting the huge coral blocks which Neale had shifted with such effort, it spat them on to the beach.

No wonder the old islanders had worshipped the power of the hurricane god.

Stacey, exhausted, slept. But it was the longest night of her brothers' lives. The raging wind did not begin to abate until the morning, but even then it blew at gale-force for the rest of the day and a lot of the night. Craig looked out at the frightening sight – debris blowing everywhere at Mach-speed, the palms twanging around like rubber toys, the sky leaden. He withdrew into the tent, which his parents had by now managed to string up between two quavering tree-trunks.

They emerged at last, cautiously, looking around. They could not believe what they saw. In the pitch darkness, they had experienced the chaos of the storm, but had no appreciation of the damage being done. Now they saw it. The island had, quite simply, been trashed. Palm trees had been torn down, banians uprooted, whole areas swept clean of vegetation.

They ventured down to the camp, anxious about some of the things – the children's schoolbooks among others – which they had abandoned there. They hardly recognized the place. Everything they'd left there seemed to have gone, blown to glory by the storm.

They all looked at Dad. His eyes were staring, looking wildly around. The skin on his face, where he had been sunburnt, was flaking off in ragged patches, which fluttered in the remains of the wind. With his two-week-old beard, he looked like something out of a horror film.

He opened his arms and let them flap back helplessly against his thighs. Then his smile came back, a smile of optimism, a survivor's smile.

'Well, kids. Well, Cath. We survived our first hurricane.'

'Our *first*?' Mum shut her eyes, as if praying. 'Dear God,' she went on, through clenched teeth, 'I don't think I could go through another one.'

The visitors

Fishing had been impossible for two days, and gathering coconuts too hazardous. All that the huddled refugees had to eat throughout the storm were a few dry crackers rescued from the camp. Now they saw their staple food was scattered all over the ground the length and breadth of the island, for the wind had done a great job of picking just about every coconut on Maina. Dozens must have been thrown into the sea, but there were dozens more simply lying around.

'Well, boys,' said Dad, still in a cheerful mood. 'You won't have to risk your necks shinning up palm trees any more. Nature's done the job for you.'

Mum and Dad began to clear the campsite, shifting the mess of fallen palm-fronds and uprooted bushes and trying to salvage some of the personal belongings abandoned in their flight to the interior. Meanwhile, the children ran up and down the beach collecting the coconuts. They brought them back and made a stockpile in a shady place, first sorting out the young, unripe ones – whose juice was best for quenching your thirst – from the mature ones, with their richer, creamier juice and flesh.

By the time they'd finished, the tent stood in its former place. With the hut gone and many trees blown away, the shade was a little less. But the banian tree had largely survived the storm.

'I'll tell you something else,' said Dad. He showed them a lump of paper, so shapeless and sodden that it had almost reverted to the pulp from which it was originally manufactured. 'This is Craig's maths book. Or should I say, it *was* Craig's maths book.'

He squashed the remains of the book between his hands and water ran over his fingers, dripping on to the ground. He turned and hurled the wet mass, like a snowball, high and far along the beach.

'Thank you, hurricane,' said Craig devoutly.

It took them three days to return to a normal life of fishing, cooking, swimming, dreaming. At first none of them could eat. The storm had shocked them out of their appetites. Then Mum issued her instructions.

'Everybody's *got* to eat a full meal today, or we'll get malnutrition and who knows what else. Tony, go fishing and bring back a big catch.'

Dad collected his gutting knife, the fish bucket and the net, and set off for a point on the other side of the island where there was always an abundance of fish. Experience had taught him that, in net-fishing, he did not really need an assistant.

He waded out into the shallow water of the lagoon, paying the net out and arranging it in such a way that he could trawl it through the water behind him. The fish were so trusting – dumb, as Matthew called them – that he got twenty or thirty in the net in this simple way, after only walking about twenty metres.

He got the catch ashore and put the net down on the sand beside the bucket. The fish, ensnared in the mesh, flashed their colours as they wriggled. He picked one out and killed it, taking the head off with a clean twist of the fingers and thumb. Then he made an incision the length of its belly and gutted it with his hooked forefinger. It was one of the small silvery fishes and they were particularly succulent, Dad thought, if you ate them raw. Mum and the children rebelled against this idea. Stacey, Matthew and Craig gagged and made vomiting noises at the very thought of it. So now, since no one was there to disapprove of him, Dad slipped the cleaned but raw fish into his mouth and chewed with relish. He even shut his eyes to enjoy the oily, slightly tough quality of the uncooked flesh. His reverie was interrupted by a strange voice.

'Hello there. I say, hello!'

The voice was a man's and the English was spoken with an accent. Dad opened his eyes in astonishment and swivelled round, squinting into the sun at the figure walking towards him along the beach.

'Hi,' said Dad at last, trying to sound casual.

The stranger was approaching from the opposite direction to the camp. He was a blond-haired young man, wearing heavily faded jeans and a polo shirt. He also wore sunglasses, canvas shoes and a baseball cap. He stopped ten metres away, a minimum distance which he kept between them throughout the short confrontation which followed. He seemed hesitant, as if poised to run. His face was a picture of disbelief.

'What are you doing here?'

He spoke good, fluent English, but it was clearly not his first language. From the way he said *here* Dad guessed the guy was German. He looked maybe twenty-five years old.

'I live here,' said Dad, still chewing his fish. He heard the children laughing distantly and turned his head. He saw them chasing each other in circles, away up the beach.

'Look,' he said. 'There's my family.'

The man didn't even glance at the children, though he must have heard them. He kept on staring at Dad, his mouth slightly open. Dad swallowed and carefully picked another fish from the net, beheading and gutting it automatically. He felt a strange conflict of emotions. He hadn't seen another human being – apart from Cath and the children – for a fortnight. And now he felt invaded. The man was uninvited, an interloper, but, as inhabitant of the island, it was his duty to give some sort of welcome and hospitality to the stranger.

On an impulse which later he couldn't explain he held out the fish.

'I've been fishing,' he said. 'Want to try one?'

The German's eyes narrowed suspiciously. He pushed out his thin lips slightly, as if about to speak. But no words came. Instead, he started walking again. His eyes were fixed on Dad, as he carefully skirted round him, keeping the distance between them. Then he continued on, hurrying along the beach towards the camp, occasionally looking back, as if to check that Dad wasn't following him. But Dad merely rose and shaded his eyes to watch the stranger's flight.

Mum and the children also watched him passing. The stranger didn't speak or acknowledge their existence, except by beginning to run when he came near them. Soon he accelerated and disappeared out of sight round the curve in the beach. They never saw him again.

'He must have been one of those yachtsmen,' said Dad. 'Yachties, they're called. They bum around the Pacific from island to island. His boat must have come in round the other side while we were asleep.'

'But why did he run away?' asked Craig.

Mum laughed. 'That's easy. He saw your dad's face.'

There was much laughter as they discussed the yachtie's strange behaviour. Afterwards they all agreed that, when he saw Dad's sun-affected, horror-film face, he must have thought it was Ben Gunn from *Treasure Island* – a crazed, marooned lunatic who might do anything to get off the island, including knock him on the head and steal his boat.

A few days later, there were more visitors, but this time they had warning. It was afternoon, with the sun just beginning to sink low enough to take the oppressiveness out of the heat. As usual, they'd been dozing through the hottest part of the day, because it was impossible to do anything strenuous. But now they had just begun to disperse to their different activities. Stacey was looking for shells for her collection; Mum and Dad had gone fishing; Matthew was playing by himself in the interior, and Craig was swimming.

Suddenly Matthew came crashing through the undergrowth and raced down on to the beach. He was pointing out across the lagoon.

'A boat, Mum! There's a boat coming.'

Matthew had been perched in a fallen tree with a view over the lagoon towards Aitutaki, and had seen a small boat with an outboard buzzing towards them.

But Mum had already seen it. Standing shin-deep in

the sea, she and Dad were shading their eyes against the glare of the sun on the water.

'How many people can you see?'

'Four, I think.'

'It might be Teré.'

They all gathered together to watch the approach of the visitors, if that was what they were. The lagoon was so flat that you could see the boat coming a long way out, but it seemed ages before they could be sure: yes, it was Palmer Marsters's boat, and two of the figures they could make out sitting amidships must be the men from the *Daily Mirror*.

The first ashore was the writer, Harry Arnold. He was a broad, middle-aged man dressed in shorts and a wide-brimmed sunhat. From his belt hung an impressive sheath knife, a weapon which would not have disgraced Tarzan. He was followed by a taller, thinner man, also in shorts. His sunhat was a similar type, made of cotton. This was the other Harry – Harry Page – who had taken the photographs of their departure from Gatwick Airport, and had now come to take pictures of their marooning. These two pink-faced men had come fresh from London in winter.

With them were Teré and Junior. They all shook hands and Harry A. explained that they'd flown in that morning from Rarotonga. This afternoon's visit to Maina was only a reconnaissance, he said, to prepare for a longer session the next day, when they would shoot a lot of film and make a video. Dad took the Harrys for a walk around the island, while Teré chatted sociably with Mum and the children. After only half an hour they were on their way again.

'We'll be back bright and early,' Harry P. called out, waving.

'And who knows – we might have some treats with us, eh, kids?' And he winked.

The next day, as promised, they were back. Harry P. was now toting several expensive, chunky cameras and Harry A. had a Minicam video camera in a black leather case.

Like hungry dogs, Craig, Matthew and Stacey watched the unloading. They had spent quite a long time last night lying in the dark and debating exactly what Harry had meant by 'treats'. In the end they agreed the expression must mean sweets – a delicious, irresistible thought after nearly a month without sugar. But the real meaning of treats was even better than their dreams of wine gums, chocolate and jelly beans. Yet what was unloaded looked, at first, a real disappointment. It seemed to be a plastic bucket.

Harry A. carried it carefully up the beach, beckoning the children over. The bucket had a lid. He raised it and they looked inside. Craig gasped.

'Ice!'

Harry was smiling, like an indulgent grandad.

'Go on, take some.'

They took a cube of ice each. In the heat, just to hold the ice was a luxurious feeling. Craig popped one into his mouth, sucking it thirstily. The others followed their big brother's example.

'Can I take another?' said Craig, innocently.

'Go ahead,' said Harry.

Craig picked a second chunk of ice, and touched it to the back of Matthew's neck.

'Yow!' said Matthew, leaping out of the way and then

dancing down the beach, waving his arms.

But it wasn't just a bucketful of ice the Harrys had brought. Underneath the delicious cold cubes were the real treats. Harry dipped down and came out with two cans of lager, gleaming wet and cold as snow. They were followed by milk shakes for the children – raspberry flavour – and then, dipping a third time, Harry was handing round ice-cream tubs.

Craig devoured his tub then and there, while Stacey took hers to Mum to have it opened. Matthew carried his reverently to a shady place, where he could enjoy it in private, savouring every too-brief mouthful as it melted on his tongue and flowed sweet and cold around his teeth and gums.

It was a hard-working day. The newspapermen wanted shots of them building a shelter, fishing, making a fire, climbing palm trees and drinking from coconuts. Harry A. particularly enjoyed using the imposing sheath knife to open his own coconuts. Harry took a lot of notes, asking them what they thought of the place, how the journey had been. He was particularly excited about the hurricane. He wanted what he called, with a big laugh, a blow-by-blow account.

The visit ended in the afternoon, after Dad had spoken directly into the video camera, reading from the big piece of paper which Harry held up for him to see. 'I've travelled thousands of miles,' he had to say, 'to live on a desert island with my family. Read about my adventures only in the *Daily Mirror*.'

And then Harry P. woke Teré, who was asleep under a bush, her head propped against an unhusked nut.

'We've just about done, Teré. Time to go?'

She looked at her watch.

'Yes, or we won't make it before dark.'

When they'd said their goodbyes and sent messages back to Swansea via the two *Mirror* men, they waved on the beach until the boat was out of sight. Suddenly everybody was very tired. They were not used to working all day through the worst of the heat.

'You know what this means, though, don't you?' said Dad, as they were eating supper. 'It means we'll be leaving Maina and going to our real desert island soon. We'll be going to Primrose any day now.'

'Why can't we stay here?' asked Stacey. 'I like it here.'

'Oh, you'll like Primrose Island more,' promised Dad. 'It's a real castaway's island. It's almost out of sight of land and everything. *Much* better than Maina.'

12

The palms of Palmerston

Within twenty-four hours the Harrys and their ice-cream became an unreal memory. It was as if this had been a visit by aliens from another planet. So now, under the hot sun and with nothing to distract them, they returned to the routines of island life. They rose early to make the most of the cooler mornings. They built huts, swam, fished, opened coconuts. Around mid-morning they took to lazing and sleeping, not becoming more active until the heat began to wane.

A little time was still given over to schoolwork, but after the hurricane destroyed most of the books and paper, it began to seem less important to be doing sums and spellings. The children had had their first taste of the awful power of nature. By comparison, reading, writing and arithmetic looked pathetic.

But at the back of all their minds – particularly Dad's – they knew that they had not yet reached the end of their journey. Maina, however much they were fond of it, was only a preparation-ground for life on the much more remote Palmerston atoll, which lay awaiting them across two hundred and fifty miles of ocean. Palmerston was a place off the trading routes, a settlement so sparsely inhabited that ships would call in there, at most, only every couple of months. So, until they got the word from Teré Marsters that a ship had come to take them there, they were confined to this halfway house.

The call came on the day – a perfect day like almost all the others – when Dad spotted the boat cutting through the water towards them, her bow throwing the sea outwards in two sparkling eyebrows of spray. A large parasol sprouted in her stern, shading the helmsman. He knew at once it was Palmer's boat. And Palmer himself, with Teré under her parasol, had come out to fetch them back.

'William has telephoned from Raro,' said Teré. 'The cargo ship *Avatapu* is on her way to us. She could be here tomorrow. Come, pack your things and we'll take you off.'

Matthew and Craig took a last look around the island as Mum and Dad dismantled the camp and Stacey gathered her collection of shells together. The boys spent a few enjoyable minutes pulling down the huts they had made, although they knew, if they'd left them, the next storm would do the job better. They took a last swim. They tried to entice Meg, Teenager and the rest of the chickens near enough for a sentimental farewell. They raced each other once all the way around the island.

And within half an hour they were chugging back across the lagoon to Aitutaki.

The next day, at Teré's house, Dad was like an ancient mariner, scanning the horizon for a smudge of smoke or a sail, or any sign that the longed-for boat was closing on the island. Three or four times he walked restlessly down to the wharf where the *Avatapu* would load and off load her cargoes. He asked for news, but there was none to tell.

Educated after the five weeks on Maina, they stocked up with an improved supply of stores from a list drawn up by Mum. It was designed to last them a long time, because their time on Primrose *motu* had no set limit.

Provisions

20lb rice
2 packets salt
15 packets dried soup
8 tins corned beef
10lb flour
1 container cabin bread
curry powder
12 toilet rolls
3 bars soap
cooking oil
3 bottles shampoo
15-gallon galvanized steel container
3 large plastic containers

Medical supplies

paracetamol
bandages
antiseptic lotion and cream
cotton wool
plasters
vitamin tablets
dehydration powder
sun lotion

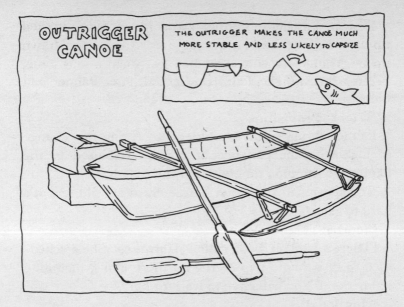

OUTRIGGER CANOE

THE OUTRIGGER MAKES THE CANOE MUCH MORE STABLE AND LESS LIKELY TO CAPSIZE

The stores were packed up in boxes and brown-paper parcels and stacked next to the luggage on the veranda of Teré's house. Then, from some outhouse, Palmer came up dragging a little blue and white outrigger canoe.

'I'm lending it to you,' he told Dad. 'Primrose is three and a half miles from the main island. Even in emergency, you can't swim it quickly.'

Dad laughed. 'Didn't you know? I can't swim at all.'

'Then you have to take the canoe. You never know.'

'Thanks, Palmer,' said Dad.

But he couldn't know just *how* thankful he would be.

The next day, there was still no sign of the *Avatapu*, in spite of more visits by Dad to the harbour. It was during one of these that, the blow fell. Palmer had gone down with him and together they'd telephoned to Rarotonga, to find out when the ship had sailed.

'She *hasn't* sailed,' Palmer was told. 'Engine's up the spout. Needs repairs.'

It was not a long conversation.

'So when *will* she sail?' Dad asked, after Palmer had hung up.

'Who knows?'

Palmer shrugged his shoulders, accepting this change of luck with the patience of a man well used to the haphazard shipping timetables of the islands.

'It happens all the time. These ships are old and it's hard to get spare parts.'

'So what's best to do?'

'There's another boat called *Martalina*. She's scheduled to do a round trip of the northern atolls, including Palmerston. You will have to wait for her.'

'How long?'

'About four weeks.'

Dad was aghast. He almost tore his hair. Who said it was better to travel than to arrive? Dad was *desperate* to arrive. Palmer saw his dismay.

'I tell you what, Tony. I'll make a few more telephone calls. You never know, we may be able to find you another way.'

Mum and the children made a tour of Aitutaki, with Dad tagging along moodily, his mind on the prospects of getting away from this island. They visited a *marae*, a sort of open-air temple surrounded by huge standing stones which had been built in pagan times, long before the Christian missionaries came to Aitutaki. All the *maraes* have stories attached to them, which tell of how and why they were first built. Aitutaki's *marae*, dedicated to Are Mangoa, the god of the sharks, came about because a certain seafarer had been wandering the ocean with a carved figure of the shark god tied to the prow of his ship. One day he noticed that the god kept moving his head, first looking one way and then, after a while, turning in another direction. The seafarer took the hint and steered his ship along the courses indicated by Are Mangoa and so was led to Aitutaki, where he founded the *marae*.

When they returned from the sightseeing trip, Palmer was waiting for them. They could see from the suppressed excitement in his face that he had news for them.

'Your problems are over. There's a boat to take you to Palmerston on her way to Mannihiki. She's leaving tomorrow. Come on, I'll introduce you to the captain.'

He took them straight down to the wharf, where they saw a rusty, oily, diesel-engined boat about thirty metres in length. A curly-haired Maori man of around forty was bending to do some work on deck. He straightened as soon as he saw them coming, waved cheerfully and leaped down on to the wharf.

'This is Junior,' explained Palmer as they came up. 'He's a pearl-diver. I've told him about you, and he's agreed to divert to Palmerston to drop you off.'

Dad thanked Junior profusely, the relief in his voice obvious even to those who found his Swansea accent a little difficult to follow. As they walked back to Teré's house, where they would spend their last night on Aitutaki, Dad's eyes were shining again. He slapped his eldest son happily between the shoulder blades and mussed his daughter's hair.

'Well, Craig, Stacey, this is it. Palmerston and Primrose, here we come!'

A couple of days later, Palmerston atoll hove into sight on the northern horizon. Discovered by Captain James Cook during his second South Seas voyage in 1773, Palmerston was not so called after the many coconut trees on the islands. Nor was it named in honour of the very distinguished British Prime Minister, Lord Palmerston, but after his now-forgotten father, who was First Lord of the Admiralty in Captain Cook's time. The atoll lies on the marine chart in the position Latitude 18° 04′ South, Longitude 163° 10′ West and has surrounding it an empty patch of Pacific Ocean, fifty thousand square miles in size.

The atoll has fifty of the Marsters family still living their traditional, precarious existence on the largest of the atoll's islands, known as Home Island. All round the twenty-mile-long reef, deserted *motus* are scattered. From time to time, and hurricane to hurricane, the number and position of these islets have changed so that visiting map-makers have counted as many as thirteen, and as few as eight, good-sized *motus* in the lagoon. Primrose, although not the biggest, is across the lagoon from Home Island and only just within sight. That is what made the place so attractive to Dad. It offered him a real feeling of solitude.

To pass by Palmerston, the pearl-fishers had deviated hundreds of miles from their planned course and they didn't want to hang around. So they suggested – instead of putting in at Home Island – they would simply drop the Williamses ashore directly on to Primrose. Dad felt a tug of regret about this. He would have liked to pay his respects to the Headman. But John James Marsters was due back on the *Avatapu* and so would not yet be home.

When he arrived, and thanks to Palmer's kindly loan of the canoe, there would probably be time enough to go and visit their friend.

They duly entered the atoll through the northern passage, well away from Home Island, and crossed the lagoon until she lay off Primrose. Craig jumped overboard and swam ashore. Dad and Mum waded, carrying Matthew and Stacey until it was shallow enough for them to wade by themselves. The stores and luggage were unshipped and brought ashore by Junior. Finally the canoe was lowered. Dad pulled it in, and beached it. By this time Junior had already meshed his gears and continued on his long voyage to Mannihiki, chugging away in a wide circle to retrace the path of foam which they had made on their way in. The children waved goodbye to the pearl-fishers, with, all around them, the luggage and stores. They waved and watched until the boat had reached its disappearing point.

'Come on,' said Mum at last. 'Aren't you going to explore? We've got to find a place for the camp.'

The island looked very like Maina. The sand was as white as paper, the sea as blue as cornflowers. If anything, though, Primrose was slightly better supplied with fruit and vegetables than Maina had been, for, as well as the inevitable coconuts, there were a few breadfruit and papaw to be had in the interior.

They found a good spot for the tent, once again on the fringe of the beach, facing north. Home Island was not in sight from here, but a line of other *motus* interrupted their view of the reef, which boomed and foamed under the unending caress of the world's largest and deepest ocean.

But as they were pitching the text, Dad made a vow.

'This time, I'm definitely building a proper sleeping hut, not just a lean-to like we had before. We've got to have somewhere more comfortable than this hellhole of a tent.'

His words were answered by a cheer from the children. They would all drink a mouthful of coconut juice to that.

13

Primrose days

It was late afternoon. Matthew left Stacey playing by herself under a tree a little way from the tent, packing sand carefully into an empty coconut shell and turning it out on the ground. Without a beach bucket, it was her way of making sandcastles, but as a matter of fact they looked more like sand-igloos. Down by the water's edge, a few metres along the shore, Mum was washing T-shirts, singing gently to herself – a hymn, it sounded like. But Mum didn't usually sing hymns, so that could have been wrong. Dad was over in his meditation spot on the other end of the island, thinking his thoughts.

Crawling along the beach on hands and knees, Matthew was trying to catch a crab. He was looking for a good specimen, because Craig had challenged him to a crab race against his own champion, a slick, fit, turbo-charged scuttler who was even now pawing the ground in his stable. The stable was a tin which Teré had lent them and which they kept at one of their play-huts, under the pandanu tree.

Unlike Maina, there was no population of wild chickens on Primrose and so, of all the land animals, the crabs were the true proprietors of this island. Looking up and down the beach, Matthew could see hundreds of small pits and holes, each one of them the daytime home of a crab. As dusk fell, the little armour-plated creatures would station themselves at their front doors, peering out until they judged it was dark and cool enough for them to take the air. By nightfall proper, the entire surface of the sand would be packed with them, thick as sunbathers on the Costa del Sol, gently clicking their pincers in the light breeze.

Most of these were the tiny hermit crabs, so called because they took up residence alone in vacant seashells – their hermitages. They could often be seen in the evening, shuffling along backwards, with their shells gripped in their claws, literally moving house by dragging it. Much bigger than the hermits were coconut crabs, which fed off fallen nuts and could grow to several centimetres across. These were rather good to eat, but very hard to

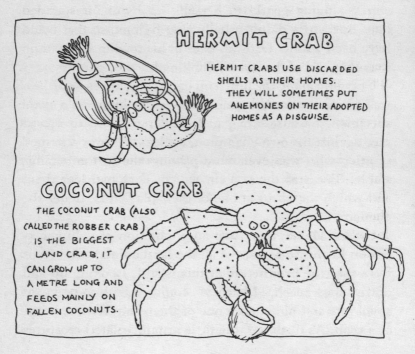

HERMIT CRAB

HERMIT CRABS USE DISCARDED SHELLS AS THEIR HOMES. THEY WILL SOMETIMES PUT ANEMONES ON THEIR ADOPTED HOMES AS A DISGUISE.

COCONUT CRAB

THE COCONUT CRAB (ALSO CALLED THE ROBBER CRAB) IS THE BIGGEST LAND CRAB. IT CAN GROW UP TO A METRE LONG AND FEEDS MAINLY ON FALLEN COCONUTS.

catch. Blessed with fast reflexes, they'd be off out of reach before your hands could close on them.

The red crabs were the most useful for racing. They were of medium size and quite easy to trap. When you saw one you simply tapped it on the shell with your finger. In alarm, it immediately withdrew its claws into the shell and you could pick it up without any danger of getting pinched. The largest of the red crabs Matthew had ever found was about seven centimetres across. Being slower, they were more exciting racers than the coconut crabs, which may seem illogical, but their comparative sluggishness made the contest longer and more full of suspense.

While Matthew searched out his runner in the crab Grand National, Craig was further up the beach, preparing the running track. He smoothed out a large area of sand and, with a stick, drew a circle about three metres across. He then placed a half coconut shell at the exact centre of the circle and went off to feed his contender. The arena was ready for the contest.

The runners could either be held in the middle of the circle by their trainers or be placed under the coconut shell. Then, on a count of *one*, *two*, *three*, came the start. The coconut shell was raised, the trainers let go of their champions, and the crabs stood for a moment blinking. Crabs hate bright sunlight and heat. When they find themselves in such a situation their instincts scream out for another place, any place so long as it is damp, dark and cool. So they scuttle. The one who scuttles first to the edge of the circle is the winner.

The play-huts had been built by the boys as places of their own, where they could store their few toys and belongings. There were two of them, each constructed roughly along the lines of a triangular tent out of branch poles thatched with fronds. One was close to the beach on the north-east side, near the place where the canoe was drawn up. The other was right in the heart of the interior, perched on the highest place of the island. The highest place was not all that high: maybe two metres above sea-level. Dad had said in an unguarded moment that a decent-sized storm wave would wash right over it. But they didn't think much about this, for the hurricane season was now over. Apart from a few heavy rain showers – gratefully caught in Palmer's metal containers to give the most refreshing drink in the world – they had been having the weather of Paradise for weeks now.

Craig checked on his champion, giving it a few crumbs of coconut meat, which it gobbled up greedily. Then he closed the lid and climbed a palm tree so he could look out across the foaming rim of the coral reef and beyond into the blue and boundless ocean. He found his mind wandering back to Wales, Swansea and West Cross, with thoughts of school and his friends. He missed his friends. Yet, with its concrete playground, its smelly changing-rooms and jostling crowd of noisy kids, that place might as well have been another planet from the one he, Craig, was on.

Looking out from his perch at the enormous emptiness of the Pacific, his tree swaying slightly in the light wind, he could well imagine himself up in the crow's-nest of some old-time naval frigate – a cabin-boy perhaps, sent aloft by the captain to spy out land. Their mission would be to explore the South Seas, like Captain Cook and the crew of his ship the *Endeavour*. The Cook Islands were named after him. Another explorer of the time was the

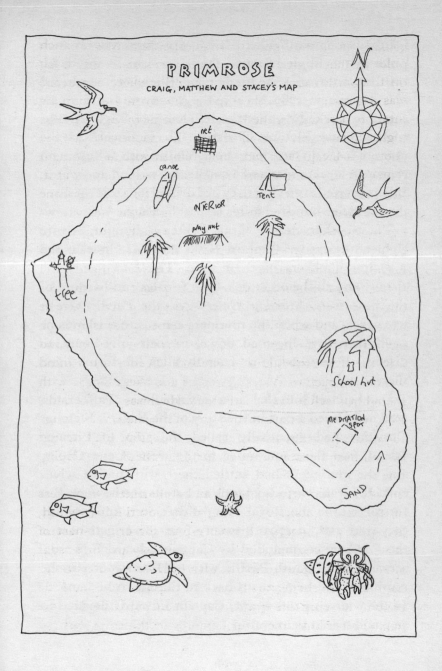

infamous Captain William Bligh, but there was no such place as the Bligh Islands, named to commemorate *his* brilliant discoveries: he made none. Bligh is remembered only because, in 1789, his ship the *Bounty* was mutinously seized by her crew under the leadership of Bligh's friend and lieutenant, Fletcher Christian. The mutineers cast the captain loose in an open boat, along with a few who remained loyal to him and a small stock of food and water. Bligh survived even after they had drifted for a total of three thousand five hundred miles across the Pacific wastes.

These characters, Craig often thought, were eighteenth-century Captain Kirks and Mr Spocks; the TV Star Trekkers of their time. The *Endeavour*, the *Bounty* and all the other oak-built frigates and barques of the time were *Starship Enterprises*, the Pacific Ocean was space, and when the mariners came across islands or atolls they were 'beamed down' in their jolly-boats, to discover if any hostile or friendly alien life-forms lived there.

Dad had told him that, in a very small way, Palmerston atoll had played a part in the story of the *Bounty*. Fletcher Christian had eventually sailed the ship to Pitcairn Island, two thousand miles to the west of the Cooks, and the mutineers had settled there with native wives collected from various islands and atolls on the way. But for some time the Royal Navy didn't even know where they were and, in 1791, a twenty-four-gun frigate named the *Pandora*, commanded by Captain Edward Edwards, arrived in the South Pacific with orders to root out the mutineers and bring them back to Europe to be hanged. In the course of this quest, Captain Edwards decided to stop and search Palmerston.

Because of the reef, the *Pandora* could not enter the lagoon, so a jolly-boat was lowered with orders to penetrate the reef and search for traces of the *Bounty* mutineers. There were only a midshipman and four able seamen on board the open rowing-boat. Suddenly a squall blew up and the frigate and jolly-boat were blown in different directions, losing sight of each other. The next few hours in the jolly-boat cannot have been very jolly. According to Edwards's log, the five men had no provisions except a single piece of salt beef. Having lost sight of his landing party, Edwards didn't try very hard to find them. He ordered his crew to sail on, and the men in the jolly-boat were never seen again. Maybe they were overwhelmed by the huge Pacific rollers and drowned. Maybe they struggled back to Palmerston, only to die there months or years later.

Twenty years on, tragedy again haunted the atoll. In 1811 a party of three Europeans led by Captain John Burbeck, with an American, a Brazilian and some Tahitians, landed on Palmerston to collect sea slugs and sharks' fins – delicacies popular for eating in Japan and China. Fourteen months later a passing ship, the merchantman *Daphne*, found a swimmer in the sea, seven miles offshore. He was dragged on board and proved to be one of Burbeck's party. There had been a fight, he reported to the *Daphne*'s master, Captain Fodger, shortly after they had landed on Palmerston. Burbeck was dead and he himself had been hiding in the bush for more than a year.

The crew of the *Daphne* were upset by what they heard. They begged Fodger to go ashore and see what had happened, but cruelly he refused. He was in a hurry, he said. He had a schedule and a cargo to deliver. So he ordered the ship to make sail, and no one ever found out just what had happened on Palmerston, or what became of the men cast away there. But in due time Fodger was repaid for his inhumanity. Several years afterwards, on a pearling expedition, he was murdered by his crew of Tahitian and Tuamotu pearl-divers.

Craig was roused from his reverie by Matthew's shout. He had caught his challenger, a nice red crab with strong-looking claws. Craig slid down the tree, collected the crab tin from the hut and raced down to the beach.

Stacey came running along the sand to watch the start. The boys put their crabs in the centre of the circle, holding them by the backs of their shells. You could not see their claws, which both crabs had prudently retracted into their shells.

'Stacey, you start the race. Count one, two three.'

'I can count more than that. I can count up to twenty.'

Craig was patient with his little sister.

'Yes, but we only want you to count up to three. Say "One, two, three, go" – OK?'

'OK. Are you ready? One, two, three, four, five –'

And then she remembered what she had to say.

'*Go!*'

The boys let go of their crabs. After a few moments of frozen suspense, Craig's runner cautiously felt the sand with his claws. Next, Matthew's did likewise. Then the crabs seemed to swivel towards and away from each other. With the claws curving out from the crabs' heads, it was something like a pair of Scottish dancers, except that this was in extremely slow motion. In reality the crabs were trying to orientate themselves, finding a direction. Then in short, nervous bursts they began their scuttle for freedom, one going north and the other south. Who would get outside the circle first? At the beginning Craig's seemed to be making better progress. It moved with steady purpose towards the boundary line and almost reached it. But then it stopped, seeming to need a breather or a pause for thought. And, meanwhile, Matthew's crab suddenly roused itself. It now clearly had urgent business outside the circle and moved off with determination. Then it, too, stopped a few centimetres short of the victory line. The trainers were not allowed to touch them or nudge them forward in any way. They jumped in the air and yelled instead. This put the crabs off even more, and they withdrew in protest inside their shells.

The issue was settled in a few seconds. As if by a turn of some switch, both crabs sparked at the same time. Smoothly engaging first gear, they performed a series of complicated scissoring movements with their legs and slid outside the circle. Nobody could tell which had crossed the line first, and the result was declared a dead heat.

14

Fever

Fish and coconuts, coconuts and fish. Grilled, boiled, barbecued, roasted, baked: however Mum rang the changes, they had to face it – the diet was getting *boring*. The rice was finished now. The dried soup was all gone, and so was the corned beef, except for one tin which Mum had kept back for a special occasion. And so it went on – for breakfast, dinner and tea: fish and coconuts, with the occasional indulgence of breadfruit and papaw, fruit which grew on the island, but in much less abundance than the palms.

But at least their bodies were getting fed. It was their imaginations that, after a few months on Primrose, had begun to starve. Since the hurricane on Maina, they had no books. The schoolbooks were destroyed, *Charlie and the Chocolate Factory* had blown away, and now, by gradual degrees, the children began to notice that they were in desperate need of *stories*.

Craig and Matthew were relentless, taxing Dad for every story, every joke, he knew. They asked him to tell them incidents from his childhood, from his time working as a school caretaker, from holidays – anything which took them mentally away from the simplicities of Primrose and into faraway places where life was more complicated and, yes, a little bit more dangerous. Sometimes Dad found the going hard.

'Tell us a story, Dad.'

'Look, I don't know any more stories. I must've told you every single story I ever heard in my life.'

'Oh, come on, Dad! Just one more. You *must* know one more story!'

Dad sighed. He tried to bluff them.

'All right, all right. Here goes. It was a dark and stormy night on the lonely island. Three pirates sat in a cave. Said one, tell us a story, Jake. So Jake began. It was a dark and stormy night on the lonely island. Three pirates sat in a cave. Said one, tell us a story, Jake. So Jake began. It was a dark and stormy night –'

'Hey, Dad! That's cheating.'

'That's not fair.'

'Give us a break, Dad.'

With Dad's stock of stories running out, Craig himself took over. He would sit cross-legged in one of the huts like an old-time storyteller, entertaining his brother and sister, sometimes using Matthew's men as props, and pulling in the characters they all knew from the *Dandy* and the *Beano*.

'So here's Dennis the Menace walking along the street. He's coming round to Softy Walter's house. Desperate Dan's come round for tea with Softy's mum and dad, but little do they know that Dennis has pushed Softy into the dish of cow pie.

'"Heh-heh," Dennis thinks, with these bubbles coming out of his head. "Softy's fallen in the cow pie, he's trapped underneath that lovely crust of delicious pastry, all covered in thick luscious Bisto gravy." But suddenly Dennis sees that Desperate Dan's going to take a bite of cow pie, so he thinks again: "Crumbs, I'd better rescue Softy now, because if I don't I won't have anybody to tease, will I?" '

Matthew and Stacey sat and listened, fascinated. They had already more or less forgotten what television was and, to them, this was every bit as good.

Even if Dad had not run out of stories, there came a time when he couldn't have told them anyway. After two days of his voice getting gradually hoarser, he woke up one morning with a throbbing, red-raw swelling lodged in his throat, which felt to him as big as a golf ball. He couldn't talk. Swallowing was agony. There was a danger that the swelling would get bigger and close his air passage, whereupon he would suffocate.

For more than a week he paced around restlessly or lay in the tent, coping with the pain. Mum made him gargle salt-water and fed him paracetamol. But the painkillers were never effective for more than a couple of hours. After eight days the illness began slowly to go away by itself.

The incident made them realize what a risk they had taken, here on this tiny island with few medicines and no help nearby. Dad's throat had nearly forced them to abandon Primrose and take to the canoe. But it was Matthew's illness that was decisive.

It started in a way that you would hardly notice. Matthew, at any rate, wasn't going to say anything about it, but he had begun to feel wobbly. At the moment, his legs didn't fancy climbing trees, his arms didn't fancy building huts, and there was a fluttering inside his chest by which he sensed he might easily burst into tears. He spent a whole day sitting in the shade, staring out to sea and playing distractedly with his men.

Mum, of course, saw that he was not himself. She came and sat beside him, put her arm around him.

'What's up, Matt? Not feeling very well?'

Matthew shook his head. He described how he felt. She put the back of her hand to his cheek and rubbed it gently up and down. She said he'd probably feel much better soon. Probably after he'd had some sleep.

But he didn't. He felt worse. Now he did cry, not energetic tears, but a gentle, sorry sobbing because he felt lousy and didn't know how to explain. The weather was hot but he felt hotter. He couldn't walk; he felt dizzy, just wanting to lie down all the time. Finally, all he wanted to do was sleep, and so he did.

Mum sat beside him in the tent, bathing his forehead with cool water. From time to time the others called in for a progress report.

'How is he?'

'Still running a temperature. He's sweating.'

'When's he going to get better?'

'Soon.'

But he didn't. Another day passed and Matthew woke up only to drink some coconut juice.

Mum was worried. She said to Dad, 'We've got to think about getting him to Palmerston. He could be seriously ill.'

'Could one of us get him there in the canoe? Leave the other with Craig and Stacey?'

Mum shook her head.

'I'm going with him, and I'm not leaving you on the island. If any of us go, we *all* have to go.'

'Well, let's see then. Give it another few hours. If he doesn't get any better, we'll *have* to go.'

And he didn't get any better. A few hours later he was

delirious. He was lying there, sweating and talking in his sleep.

'I don't want to tidy up. Please, Mum. I don't want to help Craig and Stacey. Don't make me . . .'

'What's he saying?' asked Stacey.

'A load of nonsense,' said Craig. 'His mind is wandering.'

He was looking at Mum, sitting beside Matthew. She dipped the cloth she'd been using to dampen his brow. Her face was pinched, she was frowning, concentrating hard.

Dad came up and Mum said, 'Tony, he's been like this for too long. We don't know what's the matter with him. I've got nothing to give him. He might be dying! We've got to do something.'

For a moment, Dad said nothing. He didn't want to abandon the island. He didn't want to be forced off before their time. But now he was faced with an awful choice. They could wait, maybe, a little longer. See what happened. Another twenty-four hours, perhaps. But what if Matthew *died*? His dream paradise was suddenly turned into a nightmare by the horrible, unthinkable thought. Dad knew he would never be able to forgive himself.

'Right,' he said. 'Craig and Stacey, go and get your rucksacks. Cath, you get the canoe ready. I'll carry Matthew. We're leaving right now!'

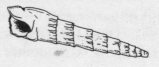

15

Across the lagoon

While Cathy and Craig held the canoe, Dad carried Matthew and placed him in the small, frail craft. They managed to wedge the suitcases in place and then Stacey got in. Dad and Mum would be sitting, with a paddle each, astride the decking. But now it was clear, there would be no room for Craig.

'We'll have to leave the luggage,' Dad decided. 'It's the only way we'll fit Craig in.'

'No need,' said Craig. 'I can swim alongside.'

'Don't be silly,' said Mum. 'You can't do that!'

'Yes I can. The water's warm. I'll stay in between the canoe and the float. I can hold on all the time.'

Which is exactly what he did.

The water was cooler out here, Craig noticed. Not chilly, like Swansea Bay, but just a degree or two off the soupy waters immediately surrounding Primrose. They had struggled two or three hundred metres out into the lagoon, with Mum and Dad paddling like crazy. Craig could hear the effort they were putting into it, because they were panting and gasping for breath.

He glanced back. How long had they been *on* the island? Craig didn't know, because they had never made an effort to keep track of the days passing. Two, three months Dad said it was. Was it now over?

A couple of minutes passed and again he looked at the island. He did this every few minutes, checking progress. He was beginning to suspect that something strange was going on. At first, they'd made good speed, pulling out from the beach towards the distant silhouette of Palmerston. But, after a while, it changed. The island they were leaving stopped getting further away, and the one they were going to stopped getting any nearer.

The problem was the undercurrent. Looking out at the glassy smoothness of the lagoon from his favourite palm tree, Craig would never have guessed there was such a current as this. It seemed to swirl one way and another, making great difficulty for the paddlers. They could not keep the canoe heading straight, for the current kept pushing the bows around. Several times they found they had gone in a complete circle. It seemed that the sea was urging the small craft to return to the beach. Or perhaps even further back, towards the line of coral reef which lay menacingly beyond the outline of Primrose.

'Craig,' Dad called out. He sounded desperate. 'You're going to have to help. When you see the bow of the canoe going off course, you've got to swim: kick your legs, I mean, while you hold on with your hands. That'll help push it back.'

They were now pointing north, whereas Palmerston lay due west of them. Craig let his legs float up under the outrigger and he kicked. He kicked again and again, and then looked. Sure enough the bow had swung a little way round to the west. Immediately Mum and Dad plunged their paddles into the water and worked hard, making several metres through the water. But now the boat was swinging in the other direction, to the south. Craig moved his legs under the canoe's hull and kicked again. This time it took longer for the craft to respond, but after five or six hard kicks, it did come round, sluggish and reluctant, to the course they wanted. Mum and Dad started working again, straining their muscles as they churned the water with their paddles. The canoe moved forward another few precious metres.

'This is going to take hours,' said Dad. 'But we've got to keep at it, or we could end up on the reef.'

At the back of his mind was the thought that, if they saw another boat, they might get a tow. But there were no other boats visible on the lagoon, no one to signal to. It looked like they were going to have to do this by themselves or not at all.

'Come on, Tony,' Mum shouted out. 'Keep paddling.'

Together they made a supreme effort, calling out all the time, *'In . . . out . . . in . . . out . . .'*

Meanwhile Craig remained always alert for the direction of travel, gradually learning the most efficient way to correct the course, first moving his legs away from the hull, then bringing them almost beneath it. And all the time he was kicking the water for dear life.

Then a wave from the bow cataracted into his face. Clearing his eyes with the back of his hand, he managed to get a look at Matthew. His brother was sitting in the bottom of the canoe, very woebegone, head in hands.

'You all right, Matthew?' Craig spluttered.

Matthew lifted his head. His eyes were open, glistening feverishly. He smiled faintly, then dropped his head again. Stacey, crouching next to him, was very still. She was also tense, Craig could tell that by the stiff way she was holding her neck and head. Meanwhile her hand was over the side, paddling the water, trying to help them along.

'Hey, Craig. Kick!' It was Dad's voice. They had swung off course again. Craig corrected the swing and Mum and Dad furiously shovelled the water. And so, centimetre by centimetre, they clawed their way towards the middle of the lagoon.

After half an hour, they began to believe that things were getting easier. The apparent magnetic attraction of Primrose and the eastern reef was weaker. The current was more consistent.

'*In-out-in-out!*'

And either Craig's job was getting less tough or he was better at it, because he had the chance to take another look at Primrose. It seemed almost incredibly small and he could hardly believe they'd been living on such a postage stamp. Amongst the bushes of the interior he could just make out the shapes of the two play-huts which he and Matthew had built. He couldn't see the tent. They had abandoned it, to save room in the canoe, but the camping place was way around the headland.

Two hours had passed since they'd set out from Primrose. The palms of Mum's and Dad's hands were raw from the chafing of the paddle handles. But Craig was still feeling pretty strong.

'Keep going,' he bullied his parents. '*In-out-in-out.*'

Now the shape of Palmerston Island was becoming much clearer. They could make out that peculiar, complicated network of fences and boundaries which criss-crossed the island, parcels of land which Dad said belonged to the various descendants of William Marsters. They could see houses, too – the same kind of simple, self-built homes they'd known in Raro and Aitutaki. They also saw something else.

'Look!' said Mum. "There's a ship in, isn't there?'

Sticking up over the hump of the island they could see the masts and superstructure of a small ship, a trading vessel, tied up at the wharf.

'Ships don't come here very often,' said Dad. 'Once every two months or so. It could be a stroke of luck.'

The sight of the ship gave them extra energy, and they paddled smoothly and strongly, with Craig still occasionally needing to kick them back on course. The frustration of the first hour was well behind them now. By comparison they were flying through the water.

'It's all right, Matthew,' called Dad. 'Soon be there now.'

They hit the beach unexpectedly, with a thud. Having paddled for five hours, they misjudged the landfall. Or they were just unwilling to slow down, because they wanted to be there as quickly as possible.

Mum and Dad were exhausted, their hands bleeding. They just sat in the canoe, breathing hard. Craig climbed over the arm of the float and staggered on to the beach. His legs felt as if they'd been beaten with a sock full of wet sand. He dropped on to his stomach, then rolled over on to his back.

'We made it. We actually made it.'

Then Dad was there, pulling him up.

'Come on, we've got to get Matthew to a doctor. Pull the canoe up on the sand.'

Mum took Stacey's hand, while Dad hoisted Matthew into his arms and strode off up the beach. Almost the first person they saw was a Cook Islander carrying what looked like a tin of engine oil.

'Excuse me,' said Dad. 'Is there a doctor on the island?'

The man looked mystified, as if he hadn't understood. That was strange, because Dad knew that English, William Marsters's native tongue, was the first language on Palmerston. He showed him the limp form of Matthew in his arms.

'Doctor! We need a doctor!'

The man smiled. They later discovered that it was Dad's Welsh accent that had baffled him.

'Ah, yes. Is the child sick? But there is no doctor here, you know. Where do you come from?'

'Back there,' said Dad, jerking his head. 'Primrose Island.'

The man's eyes opened wide.

'On the *motu*? What were you doing there?'

'Living there. But what are we going to do if there's no doctor? My son's got a bad fever.'

The man smiled again. His puzzlement hadn't completely gone away, but it was mixed with pleasure. He reckoned he would be able to help them out.

'No problem. I am the engineer on that ship over there. You can come with us, we're going to Rarotonga today. You can see the doctor in Rarotonga.'

'When do you sail?'

'In an hour. You've come just in time.'

They boarded the small freighter without delay, crouching under a canvas awning on deck, as they had during their two previous sea voyages. Dad and Craig went back to collect the luggage from the canoe. They received strange looks from some of the Palmerston islanders they passed.

'What'll we do with the canoe, Dad?'

'Can't take it with us. Captain says there's not enough room. Anyway it really belongs in Aitutaki, not Rarotonga. So we might as well leave it here.'

Craig touched the skin of the canoe as if he were saying goodbye to it. After all, it had just about saved them.

'Come on,' said Dad, looking at his watch. 'Ship sails soon. We've got to go.'

Craig and Stacey didn't think they'd ever forget the feeling of concrete under their feet again. The concrete was on the quay at Rarotonga, when they leaped from the deck to the dockside. It felt so solid and unbreakable that they jumped up and down on it like pogo-sticks.

This was two days after they'd sailed from Palmerston. Matthew had begun to make a slow recovery during the trip, helped by the crew and other passengers making a great fuss of him. So by the time they reached Raro, he was pale and weak, but could just about walk. Within a few minutes of coming ashore, they were asking directions to Dr Woonton's surgery.

'Is he better than he was?' said the doctor. He was checking Matthew's pulse.

Mum nodded.

'Probably nothing but a virus. He's on the mend, I'd say. But I'll give you a prescription.'

He patted Matthew on the head, reached for his pen and prescription pad, and scribbled briefly.

When Mum and Dad returned to the doctor's waiting-room, bringing Matthew and his prescription, they found Craig and Stacey standing in front of a large, glass water-cooler, its exterior gleaming with condensation. As they took turns to pour themselves cups of the stuff, they agreed with each other: it was just about the most delicious, cool, *wicked* drink they had ever had in their lives. Craig poured one for Matthew, and he drank it clean down in one swallow, his eyes shining.

16

Home

It doesn't take long to tell the end of the story. The family stayed another week with William Richards, who again offered to adopt the three children, or at least take them into his house while Mum and Dad returned to Wales to get their book published.

'After that you can come back and go again to Primrose,' he said with a flash of his biggest smile.

Mum and Dad refused the offer. They knew it was sincere and kindly meant, but they said they'd got used to having the children's faces knocking around the place, and they reckoned they'd miss them.

And then began the long haul back to Gatwick.

Swansea in summer felt cold and wet. Nanna and Bampa didn't know they were coming back, so to give them a surprise the children put on grass skirts and wrap-around skirts known as *pareus*, carried Cook Island spears and Tangaroa figures. Then they went and knocked at the door.

When Nanna opened the door she didn't recognize her own grandchildren. She thought it was some prank by the local children and was all ready to shoo them away when Craig said, 'Hello, Nanna.'

Then Nanna screamed with joy, really screamed. All the neighbours must have heard. It was like the signal for the start of celebrations.

Later, seated by the fire, Bampa had a quiet word with Dad.

'You're not going back to that place, are you?'

Dad didn't speak at once. He studied his hands, then looked at Bampa seriously.

'Yes,' he said. 'I think so. I think we are definitely going back. And this time, we'll stay a *really* long time.'

'Oh.' Bampa said nothing more. With a shake of the paper, he turned back to the sports page. But Craig noticed that he was holding the edge of the paper with a *very* tight grip.

If you want to read more . . .

The loneliness and beauty of the South Sea islands have appealed to our imaginations ever since the first explorers (or 'Star Trekkers') went there from Europe in the 1600s and 1700s. The first and greatest of all books about castaways in the South Seas is, of course *Robinson Crusoe* by Daniel Defoe. Almost as popular over the years have been *The Swiss Family Robinson* by J. D. Wyss and *The Coral Island* by R. M. Ballantyne. All three are available as Puffin Classics.

These books are adventures which try to show the challenge of life on the islands and how the castaways triumph over them. A much sadder – but still terrifically exciting – story on the same theme is *Lord of the Flies* by William Golding, where a planeload of young schoolboys crashes on an island. The pilot and crew are killed, which leaves the boys to fend for themselves, with somewhat grisly results.

If you want a factual account of a twentieth-century castaway's life, you could search out Tom Neale's story of being alone on Suwarrow, one of the Cook Islands, called *An Island to Oneself*. This is not, as far as I know, still in print, so you will have to go to a library or try second-hand bookshops.

An entertaining account of life in another Pacific island group, similar to the Cook Islands, is given in Arthur Grimble's *A Pattern of Islands*.

P.H.